The
L·A·D·I·E·S

DORIS GRUMBACH

FAWCETT CREST • NEW YORK

A Fawcett Crest Book
Published by Ballantine Books
Copyright © 1984 by Doris Grumbach

Library of Congress Catalog Card Number: 84-5999

ISBN 0-449-20818-4

This edition published by arrangement with E.P. Dutton, Inc.

Manufactured in the United States of America

First Ballantine Books Edition: September 1985

The LADIES

FOR MY FRIENDS:

Joseph Caldwell
Tristram Coffin
Gilbert Harrison
Roderick MacLeish
Faith Sale, who gave me the first right steer
May Sarton, who talked to me about the Ladies
Hilma Wolitzer, who read the manuscript with a cool eye
and Allan Gurganus, to whose fine ear I first confided
    this story

"Madame, all stories, if continued far enough, end in death, and he is no true story-teller who would keep that from you. Especially do all stories of monogamy end in death."

—ERNEST HEMINGWAY
Death in the Afternoon

APOLOGIA

Writing about the Ladies in *Ces plaisirs* in 1932, Colette apologized for sinning against chronology: "I reverse the order, and I do not excuse myself at all!" My offenses against the Ladies' histories are far greater. I have changed names, switched facts about, changed and abridged the chronology, inferred, interpreted, denied, imagined. This is *a fiction* about the Ladies of Llangollen, not in any way a history. I have 'made them up' as I imagine they might have been. Like Colette, I do not excuse myself at all.

IRELAND

1739–1778

*S*he stands looking out the long window, the toe of her silk slipper hard against the sill. She holds her back painfully straight, trying to imagine what it will be like tonight in stirrups, in the saddle. Outside, the wet day is sliding fast into clouded night. There will be no moon for her ride.

She calculates that it is almost four o'clock. Behind her, in the long hall lined with blackened portraits of her ruffed and wasp-waisted Ormonde forbears, she thinks she hears Milligan moving towards her mother's rooms. He will, as usual, inform her mother that dinner will be served. Always it is 'will be,' allowing her mother time to traverse the long hall to her father's dressing room. Her mother will help her father to his feet and lead him, now that his vision has narrowed to a blurred stream of fitful light, towards the small eating room where the three now have their dinner.

This is her last evening. When it is quite dark, when the

3

vast, untidy park she is staring at now, without quite focussing upon the rough tumps and the obtrusive birse, turns blue, then black, and then merges with the lowering Irish sky, when the Nore River at the edge of their land mells with the blotched demesne and the hooded sky: then she will go, saying farewell to her dog Lento, leaving behind Kilkenny Castle and the whole company of servants, cotters, neighbors, and relations she has always known.

She considers what it will be like not to walk beside the quicks of the hedges in bud, never again to see the quiet, undersized Irish cattle that graze their fields untended, the birth of each white-faced calf a day's or night's excitement in eventless lives. Not to roam the bracken of the hillsides, wading the stretches of bog, stirring up partridge from the hollow, pheasant out of the stubble. Not to witness the strained, worshipping posture of her mother, everlastingly at prayers in the chapel at the end of her sleeping room. No more to hear her high-pitched fulminations at the servants for oversleeping, at the cotters for their absence from castle Mass in order to work their cabbage gardens, threatening them violently, as always she has, with hunger, loss of shares, and everlasting perdition. Nor her high voice badgering her daughter for not marrying, not improving her father's chances of regaining his title, lost to him by a treasonous forbear. To leave behind the sight of her father's bulbous hands as he raises them, needing both to guarantee the elevation of the after-dinner port glass to his lips without accident, his cravat dotted with bits of salt beef and orange preserve where the napkin has failed to catch what his gums can no longer retain. To not witness the downing of the entire contents of the port decanter and then his struggle for upright dignity as he makes his way to his rooms between her angrily dutiful mother and Milligan.

They have been her life and her company since she was allowed to leave the convent school at Chambrai, since her younger sister married and went to live on her husband's estate. At thirty-nine, she is a blank and useless maiden to her aging parents, who grow increasingly ill-tempered, religious, and disappointed with their lives and with hers. They are no longer compelled by the needs of their daughters for sympathy and care, and so no longer capable of them. Preoccupied with their failing memories, too selfish and too proud to want old friends to witness their declining patience, health, and capacity for affection, they lean to each other, for the first time in their married lives, and away from everyone else, away from her.

Only yesterday her mother informed her of her plans. She had heard them before but never had they seemed so well developed, so unalterable. To her mother's priest-dominated mind her daughter was to be an offering to the Faith, a sacrifice, human recompense for her own brother's desertion to the Established Church. She, who yearned for freedom and the full, unchained play of her hungry mind and restless body, was now destined to return to the Chambrai of her pious education, or better, her mother hoped, to the Convent of the Holy Sepulchre at Liege, an exclusive yet laudably inexpensive place for an aging daughter with a limited, three-hundred-pound dowry. In her mother's view, Chambrai or Holy Sepulchre had all the virtues of heavenly ransom and domestic economy. Her daughter's maiden state, withering and stale in her sight, would be stowed away suitably, permanently, among sacred, believing virgins.

From behind closed eyes she watches them seat themselves beside each other, their trays placed side by side at the end of the square mahogany board so that her mother may cut her father's mutton chop and arrange the gravy in wells of cheesed potatoes. Her mother will ask Milligan to fetch Lady Eleanor. When she is not to be found in her room, Milligan will dispatch a maid, perhaps Mary, to search the state rooms. She will look first in the upstairs parlour where often Eleanor reads.

'Please, m'lady. Dinner is already served.'

She is not yet a Lady, not until the dukedom of Ormonde is again her father's. But her parents insist the servants use their titles-that-may-be, so determined are they on the eventual restoration.

'Please, m'lady . . .'

She does not turn. She fears, curiously, that Mary will read her plan to escape in her face, in the way she holds her lips to conceal the pleasure she feels at the prospect for this night.

'Tell my father I am somewhat unwell and shall not dine. Perhaps something later, on my tray, upstairs.'

She listens to Mary's departing steps, the linen slippers her mother orders for the serving people (so their soundless passage will polish the bare-board floors) making short, repetitive shushes in the hall. She is nervous and very excited: her plan is to leave by a side door as her parents linger over the port. She is relying on the slow service, the distance the servants come from the kitchens and pantries, pushing dollies laden with tureens and serving dishes, and on the long way they must return to fetch the pudding, the cheese. She counts on the slowness of their eating, their sipping of the wines, her mother mincing the half a chick or the parsnips and salad for her husband's consumption, their profound attention to each bite, as though they wanted to diminish the time between this mouthful and the last.

Far away, she believes she hears the sounds of overtaxed wheels grinding rustily along the lower hall. The broth and bowls are returning to the pantry. Not looking back to verify her supposition, she opens the long door as quietly as she can, pushes Lento down with the instruction to sit, steps over the sill, and walks very quickly across the wide stone porch until she reaches the bench under which her chambermaid Ellen has said she would hide the riding clothes.

O delight! the bundle is there. The breeches are old and spotted and will not fit, she thinks, but no matter. She knows it is coming on to dusk, but she pretends it is truly dark and so disregards her half-dressed state. She finds the jacket and puts it on over her chemise, leaving only her scarf to be crushed into the collar as a neck cloth. She leans against the rough trunk of the beech tree that shades the porch to put on the boots, and rolls her skirts and shoes and petticoats into a tight ball, bestowing them in the same spot that harboured the habit. There she finds gloves and the whip that Ellen told her were in the old stables. (How kind! How busy she has been on her behalf!)

The boots are much too tight, the waistband on the breeches will not buckle, but she is so eager to be gone that she pays no heed. She stumbles along as fast as she can, staying close to the shadow of the high walls that have shielded Kilkenny Castle for centuries against the threats of hut-dwellers' fury and the assaults of brutal Irish winds. She will be without their protection now: she senses for the first time what it will be like to be deprived of the safety of family and the support of hereditary walls, to be free to be the woman she has kept well hidden for so long.

From the low dark outline of the old stables, long ago bereft of grooms, tackle, carriages and horses, she hears the neigh of the horse Ellen has arranged to be waiting for her. Its owner, she was told, is an ostler in the town who hires out to travellers. Ellen has instructed him to stay with his animal in order to assist Eleanor in mounting. There have been no horses in these stables for many years, ever since her father was tossed during a cross-country ride, shattering his anklebone and his elbow, his head struck into unconsciousness against a stile. Furious at the horse's clumsiness, he ordered all the horses sold, the carriages stowed away, and the grooms and drivers transferred to castle and grounds duties. Now, when her parents want to travel, they hire a chaise from the village. But it is a long time since they have wished to do so.

She is guided to the dark stable door by the sound of hoofs stamping in place, by a horse's deep, rattling snort.

'Over here, m'lady,' she hears.

There is light from a lantern. By it she sees a man and a horse. His one hand holds the bridle, the other is on the horse's flank as though to calm him. In her excitement at leaving at last, she has forgotten how frightened she is. But now, when the horse snorts again and stamps under the man's hand, her heart pounds, her hands become wet. The tight heavy boots cut into her ankles like flame. She thanks the man who lowers his lantern so she is able to see moving restless hoofs, the man's blunt-shod feet, her own painful boots, the stirrup.

He reaches for her arm, as she puts her left foot into the stirrup. She feels sodden with fear and clothes. He lifts her up and her knee makes a snapping sound as she swings her leg over the broad back of the horse. The animal is black and bigger, it appears to her, than any horse she has ever seen. She is full of anxiety at the prospect of the black night, the tortuous roads she is only faintly familiar with even in light, the huge, restive horse. The man settles the bridle on the horse's head and gives her the reins.

His hand on the bridle, the man leads her through deep grass to the path, which looks, from her elevation, like a bottomless ribbon, darker than the laurel hedgerows, narrower than the yews that close over her. Her hands grip the reins so hard she can hear her knuckles crack over them. Her knees are clenched against the horse's flanks, almost one with the stirrup's leathers. She manages to thank the ostler for his help, afraid to take her eyes from the road ahead to look at him, praying she will find her way in the dark, that she will not be stopped by the villainous Whiteboys who attack priests, tax collectors, and well-to-do travellers. But in the dark and in these clothes, she thinks, she will not be taken for a prosperous person. Only one thing—the thought of her beloved at the end of this fearful journey—propels her forwards. There are fifteen miles to travel, over roads made of unbroken stones and mud, to the barn near Woodstock where they have arranged to meet.

She has never been on a horse before.

The couple, alone in the vastness of Kilkenny Castle, had waited years for the arrival of an heir. In despair, Lady Adelaide fell into a nondescript illness and took to her bed. For the first time since their betrothal it became possible for Lord Walter to visit her in her chamber in the early hours of the afternoon when his vital energies were still his to summon and before his resort to the supper port, claret, and brandy debilitated him. The outcome was heartening to them both: Lady Adelaide found she was pregnant.

Eleanor was told her father had actually smiled when his wife informed him of the news. His smile came so rarely that the two deep ruts between his eyes never smoothed out, the descending lines at the sides of his mouth were almost permanent.

'We have great need of a son,' he said, smiling at his wife.

She understood. His effort to restore his Ormonde title had been his life's main concern. She too yearned for a boy, understanding the salutary effect of a hereditary male presence upon households such as theirs, upon the keepers of the preserves, the tenants. Knowing how ineffectual was her lazy, tun-shaped husband, Lady Adelaide idealised a slim, strong young body energetically pursuing his parents' affairs, a curly haired, judicious head, a bright, compassionate spirit who would assure protection to her aging person (for surely her wheezing, goutish husband would 'go' before her). Hers would be the final comforts of a son's mother-love. She thought of the pleasures of childbearing in religious terms. Her Catholicism was firm and sentimental: at long last she would fulfill the blessed example of the fruitful Holy Mother and bear a son.

From her mother, Eleanor came to believe that Lady Adelaide's lying-in was the happiest time the Butler family was ever to know. His Lordship managed to turn his attention from the ancient wrongs done his family by George the First (James Butler's title, the Duke of Ormonde, had been summarily removed, his honours extinguished, his estates forfeited, for a nameless act of high treason). Freed of this concern for the moment, Walter Butler was able to manage a modicum of solicitude for his wife's condition. On one occasion, he brought a cushioned chair close to the fire for her use. He took care to carve thin mutton slices to save her the exertion of using her knife. Frequently, he buttered her scones. He went so far as to allow her to precede him to table, disguising his normal gluttony in a cloak of paternal concern and anticipation.

'He will make our days a great pleasure,' Lady Adelaide told her husband at table.

His Lordship grunted his agreement without ceasing to chew. His eagerness for the coming event took no verbal form. Under ordinary conditions, he spoke rarely to anyone but the cook, his valet, his manager, and then only in an adjuratory tone. But his purchases in the months before the event were evidence of his secret delight: a pair of small brogues, a miniature gun with chased-silver barrel and stock, a curly coated grey pony. Lady Adelaide showed her delight by ordering from Sheffield of London two silver porridge bowls and a crooked-necked silver spoon, the letters *SON* to be embossed upon the handle.

On the night of the expected birthing, after two aged but skilled midwives had arrived from Dublin, the castle's gates were locked and all the doors barred. These were extraordinary measures, taken to protect the precious heir. They remained closed for two days while poor Lady Adelaide, now in her thirtieth year, struggled feebly to rid herself of the reluctant baby she had so joyfully awaited. Her agonized cries could be heard by maids in the distant pantries. In sympathy, they covered their ears with hands sour from pan scouring. Wet sheets and bloodied cloths were carried in basins from her chamber past Lord Butler seated heavily in a chair in the hall before his rooms. His brows contracted at the sight of them. Hearing his wife's high, gasping cries, his head sank over his brandy glass.

'Can nothing be done to hasten matters?' he asked the

midwife when she passed through the hall on her way to the kitchen for her belated supper, bearing with her a basin of foul-smelling liquid.

'Soon. Soon, m'lord.' She did not stop to allay the poor husband's anguish. Her business was with the suffering woman, she believed, not with the self-indulgent pleasure-seeking cause of it all. Lord Butler sank back in his chair. He had convinced himself that the rooms full of women attending his wife were paying far too little attention to the welfare of his still unborn son. He muttered to himself: 'All those women using up the air in there,' without being aware that his poor labouring wife was included in the usurptive sorority.

At dusk of the third day it was all over. Attendants poured out of the chamber, jostling each other in their efforts to be the first to inform Lord Butler of the happy news, the arrival of a fine, sturdy, healthy baby. Lady Adelaide lay inert in their great bed, still flooding it with blood. So great was the excitement of those surrounding the screaming baby, very large and long and equipped with a head of spiky black hair, that Lady Adelaide was left to herself for the first minutes of the baby's life. The noise in the alcove where the baby now lay was deafening. Lord Butler joined the celebrating group and tried to ask his pressing question, to no avail. Above the sounds of footsteps coming and going, rustling skirts, exclamations of admiration and delight from the crowding women-attendants, the high resentful cry of the newborn child rose, shrill and strong.

Excitement spread. In celebration, the guns of gameskeepers and fowlers were fired at the edge of the park. The bewildered father and his bleeding wife alone seemed untouched, he overwhelmed by the confusion around him, she exhausted by the brutal birthing. When the attendants finally departed, the baby quieted, Lord Butler was able to bring himself to approach his wife's bedside. He found her spent but awake. He stood at a little distance, fearful of the sight of her pain.

'Is our son well?' she whispered.

'I think so,' he whispered, bending towards her, looking over his shoulder at the mammoth, lace-draped cradle in the distant alcove. No sound came from it.

'See,' she managed to command, with her last energy. Then she dozed off.

The baby lay still, tired out by its first violent protests at the indignities of birth, its large head on a satin pillow, whirls of lace above and tufted white quilting over its plump body. Lord Butler's need overcame his fear of the unfamiliar, curious creature. He reached deep within the folds of blue coverings, removing layer after layer of the soft stuff that encased the sleeping child until he reached its raw, flaking flesh. He saw a still-bleeding stump protruding from its belly, and then the small, neat seam between its fat thighs. Lord Butler's cheeks reddened dangerously. He looked ready to burst into flame. Roughly he pushed the garments and coverlets back into place.

'No!' he shouted. The expelled monosyllable sounded like a small explosion. 'No!' he said again. He backed away from the cradle. Lady Adelaide awakened in fright. He saw her swollen, blackened, questioning eyes, but he could not prepare an answer. Instead, he turned and rushed from the room without saying anything to her, leaving her immobile and terrified among the wet bedclothes, wondering what she had done, whether he was angered by her long travail, which must have occupied the entire attention of everyone at Kilkenny to the disruption of his usual routine, or—the unthinkable for her at this moment—whether the baby was deformed in some way. Worn out and confused, she fell back to sleep.

Outside, Lord Butler stood facing the standing hall mirror, recognising his coarse, red features as enlargements of the baby's. He concentrated on bringing his shaking flesh and clenched, shocked hands under control. Seated again in the chair he had occupied for most of the past three days, he held his head in his hands. In his mouth was the burning, acid taste of the terrible feminine common noun: a *girl*.

On her seventh birthday Eleanor learned from her nurse, Miss Colum, that she was a girl. For years Lord Butler's disappointment with her sex had been somewhat appeased by the child's absence from his sight, and her deceptive appearance on the rare occasions when he did catch a glimpse of her. She ran after balls or rode beside the nurse in the pony cart, dressed in Irish woollen knickers and vest, a white linen shirt, and miniature cravat. The boy's clothes, and the glow of her close-cropped red curls, helped to mollify his choler. If she were not a boy, to him she was at least a credible semblance of one. Her slim, wiry athletic body in its boy's accoutrements advanced the illusion for her father. As for Eleanor, she did not require the illusion. She never doubted she was male.

'I will explain it to you once again,' Miss Colum said. 'There *is* a difference.'

'What is it then? What is the difference?'

Miss Colum's stern grey face revealed her Irish puritanism, which prevented her from offering a detailed explanation, and certainly not a description. She thought a moment and then said, 'Girls have long hair, wear gowns and petticoats, slippers and sashes and hair ribbons. And,' she hesitated, 'are made differently.'

'In what way? Where?'

'On their chests—and between their legs.' Miss Colum's discomfort at the questions showed in the spots that appeared on her cheeks. Pushed to definition, the end of her nose became cherry-coloured, her eyelids and chin an unaccustomed ruddy hue.

Eleanor asked nothing further. She saw no problem in the whole matter. It was clear now to her: 'If I do not allow my hair to grow I will never be a girl,' she told herself. 'If I refuse to wear dresses as ladies do, I will always be a boy.' As for the other, less well-defined differences, her fine flat chest and the bare opening between her legs for her necessary occasions: surely these places could make no difference. They would be well hidden from public view by her shirts and knickers. She would be a boy, and then a man. She saw no difficulty at all.

In her room, left to herself when Miss Colum went off for visits to the servant's quarters, and after a long day of play and pretending, she cut her hair close to her head. For this purpose she used the hunting knife she had found in the stables and kept from Miss Colum's eyes under the toy chest. The curls she cut off were saved in a tin box. To her mind they served as talisman against the sex she had abnegated. Preserved in this way, her curls could be controlled and would not reattach themselves, she believed, especially since she took care to keep the tin box tightly closed. Regular shearing would prevent excessive growth, she believed, and would guarantee her chosen sex.

It is hard to know if the girl-child born to Lord and Lady Butler and named, in the fourth week of her life, Eleanor, would have demanded boy's clothes and cropped hair had they not been first accorded her by her deeply disappointed parents. No effort was made to replace the wardrobe and toys prepared for their son before her birth. Lady Adelaide's frail health kept her from influencing her daughter's wardrobe even had she wished to. As it was, she desired only to be freed of responsibility for her so that she might concentrate her whole attention on her own uncertain health and her private devotions to the Holy Mother and Her Blessed Son. She hardly noticed Eleanor's clothes when she was brought to table to say good-night at the start of supper, dressed carefully in velvet knickers, Eton spencer, a sparkling white shirt, and linen stock.

As Eleanor grew older, Miss Colum complained to the cook, she was given 'the run of the place.' She stayed away from the castle for hours, exploring the demesnes and the hills beyond, running through the fields of furze, the meadows filled with foxglove and buttercup, returning only for meals and to sleep.

Until she was eleven, Eleanor was that oddity among children, a contented solitary. She grew tall, her shoulders broadened, her waist thickened, her legs formed straight and thick. To her delight, her breasts remained rudimentary, and her hands and flat sturdy feet were larger than most boys'. Outdoors, far from the sight of those in the castle, she donned her 'play' costume, heavy leathern boots and cut-down breeches left from her father's riding days. She wound a thick cashmere scarf about her throat and covered her hair with a woolen tam. Otherwise, she made no concession to the wild, cold Irish wind. Miss Colum was lethargic, short-legged, flat-footed, and did not attempt to follow her charge on her excursions. Eleanor never discussed the contents of her solitary games with her, or with anyone, for that matter. Where she went, what she did was known only to herself. Her pursuits were full and sustaining, enough to make her happy and occupy an essential part of her days. When she finally appeared at half after three before her nurse to be made presentable for her appearance at supper she would be muddy and weary, but exultant.

'Ride, harder,' she told the gaunt stone lion, one of a pair that guarded the farthest gate near the old stables. Her knees numb from the cold (for she always removed her breeches) she rode him hard, rocking forward and back on his broad boney back, leaning out perilously from his sides, feeling him move under her. The pleasures of her ride rose up in her until, at their height, she screamed. Her delight filled her whole body. When her ride was over (a journey she took two or three times a day in all weather), she climbed down slowly and whispered her gratitude into the lion's stone ear. She rescued her breeches from her secret hiding place between his haunches and put them on. Lovingly, she moved her hand over his back.

'You are all wet,' she said to him, convincing herself he was capable of furious sweat, never allowing herself to believe that in her ecstasy it was she who had dampened his granite back.

When Eleanor was twelve another daughter was born to Lady and Lord Butler. This time there was no disappointment, for the couple had been afraid to hope. The baby was named Margaret. She grew up adoring Eleanor but too distant in years and too different in nature to be influenced by her sister's boyish posturings. Margaret was small, blonde, and nervous, afraid of the garden snakes that seemed to stalk her during outdoor games while ignoring her sthenic sister, who liked to catch the slippery creatures and hold them before her little sister's skittish eyes. Except to frighten and to tease her, Eleanor left the child entirely alone. Soon after Margaret's second birthday Miss Colum was transferred to her care, to the nurse's disguised delight: little Margaret was pretty and biddable, undemanding and dull. Her parents had decided it was time to have Eleanor instructed by someone possessed of more than the elementary capacities of the governess.

The tutor hired away from a Dublin family, Theo O'Phelan, was a serious and delicate young man. His arms were long and very thin, his wrists and hands protruding from his coat as though dangled from strings. His face looked perpetually frostbitten. In his inadequate clothes, he seemed never to have experienced bodily warmth. His boots were too tight, so he walked with a curiously extended gait, his feet thrown out at variance to each other. Eleanor sometimes amused herself by shadowing him. She imitated his walk by extending her hands and feet at incongruous angles. Always irreverent, she called him Theodore, a name he disliked. But he was so in awe of the Butlers, even of their fourteen-year-old daughter, and the general aura of Kilkenny Castle, that he never reproved her. A theology student at Trinity College in Dublin, he paid his tuition with the money he earned by tutoring. His belief in God was intense: His Name appeared in some part of speech in many of his sentences, his seemingly disembodied hands appeared to be invoking His Presence in the air.

Eleanor hated the idea of being tutored, most particularly by Theo O'Phelan. He was too much like a girl, too soft, quiet, easily bent and swayed, too physically awkward. Her fingers were more dextrous than his, and she easily outran him the few times she had been able to persuade him to race with her. Once, in mid-race, he stumbled and fell over the root of a tree. She returned to offer him her hand, feeling strong and manly, and he took it. But he was well-educated, he taught her to recite Burns and Wordsworth and Cowper and Donne, to read French, to conjugate Latin verbs. They started to study Greek, but she balked at the long list of irregular verbs, so he surrendered on this point. Once lessons were over, however, Eleanor could not persuade the tutor to go further from the house than the stone porch. He disliked everything about the outdoors and would accompany her only on formal, stated afternoon walks if the weather was exceptionally fine. She believed he felt threatened by the overgrown hedgerows.

'You are a true baby,' she told him.

He denied this, but there was some truth in Eleanor's conviction about his fear of the great towering ash and beech trees that arched towards each other along Kilkenny Castle roads. They terrified him, as much as a bird rising quickly out of a grassy hollow. He would not walk at the back of the castle where laurel and hawthorn hedges grew thick and broad, preferring to follow the edges of meadows and greens. All his life he had lived in a Dublin row house, a low, narrow structure comfortably supported on both sides by another house just like itself. Such snug buildings, their facades facing honestly to the street with no intervening greenery between them and the brick street, their rear ends aligned similarly in communal sameness with a bit of green as big as a square of paper behind them, and all without sides or obscure entries or exits, made him feel entirely safe.

Most of all, Theo O'Phelan hated the loud noises peculiar to the countryside. Fowlers' guns sounding in the game preserves startled him, causing his head and hands to tremble. With each succeeding explosion his tremors grew stronger until it seemed as though his whole body were possessed. On these occasions, Eleanor was cruel, calling him Saint O'Vitus, and laughing while he shook. If he was not able to stop, she grew quickly bored by the cowardly spectacle and went off without him to her own pursuits. When they met again, at supper, she would lecture him, to the amusement of her parents or guests, on the arts of hunting, fishing, and fowling, hoping he would reproduce his bizarre behaviour at table at the very suggestion of guns exploding.

Eleanor would have liked to have her lessons outdoors in fine weather, but O'Phelan would not hear of it. He insisted they study in the dark panelled library, surrounded by heavy oak tables, portraits of the dukes of Ormonde already almost blackened beyond identification by the huge fire built in the library, and walls hung with tapestries to hide cracks and crevices. Here O'Phelan felt secure; here Eleanor felt closeted and bound in. She learned her lessons as quickly as possible in order to escape outside. Prepared to make a quick departure, she lounged in a cushioned library chair in her rough stable boy's clothing, her boots resting on the table, while O'Phelan sat behind a small desk asking questions to which she replied scornfully but always correctly. Freed from the four hours' confinement, the time allotted to languages, mathematics, and literature, she left without a word. Outside, she plotted every sort of revenge upon the fearful tutor, elaborate tricks to show what a goose-livered girl he was, what a courageous man she was becoming. Oddly it was her mother, hardly aware of the tutor's existence, who, without intention, effected Eleanor's freedom from the theology student. In this way:

One late afternoon in the coldest month of that year 1755, Lord Butler sat at the head of a long dining table at which the local gentry as well as guests from some distance from Kilkenny were assembled. Once or twice a year such hospitality was offered at the castle. At that time all its heavy but splendid furnishings were displayed, a footman in livery placed behind every chair, a feast of meats and fish and puddings and fruit served, with a constant supply of wines of every variety. Still suffering under the illegality of his title and the degradation of his loss of ancient rank, Lord Butler (as he called himself always) sat enthroned in his cushioned chair at the head of the table. Because Lady Adelaide was not up to her duties as hostess that evening, sixteen-year-old Eleanor, in one of her mother's old, stiff, richly brocaded gowns, occupied the foot. In a rare moment of thoughtfulness, Lady Adelaide had invited the tutor to be present. Theo sat huddled into himself, looking to neither side, his eyes fixed on his downturned glass. For he did not drink, knowing the effects of liquor on his weak nervous system.

To the tutor's left was Beauchamp Bagenal, Member of Parliament for bordering County Carlow. Bagenal was a man of generous proportions and more than generous appetite. He ate and drank so steadily that he had little time to talk at table. Downing a generous mouthful of wine after every swallow of food, Bagenal paid no attention to the conversation, which, this evening, centered about the rumored escape to a convent of a duchess. Her husband and other indignant noblemen had broken into its locked confines to retrieve, not the duchess, but her property. The tutor was appalled at the roars of approving laughter that greeted this irreverent story. He fixed his indignant stare lower to the table. So he failed to notice that Beauchamp Bagenal had placed a brace of pistols beside his plate. When dinner was finally over, the ladies retired, all but Eleanor, who did not consider herself one of them and exercised the hostess's privilege of remaining seated. Milligan entered the dining room with a new cask of claret.

'Over here, oul' man,' the Member of Parliament called at Milligan, who circled the table to deposit the cask before Bagenal. With a gesture so wide that his elbow grazed the oblivious tutor's head, Bagenal picked up a pistol in his left hand, aimed it precisely at the side of the cask, and tapped it with a bullet. Milligan, seemingly well-prepared for the guest's gross act, quickly held a glass to the flow, but not before a blood-red puddle had filled the table in front of the marksman and the tutor. So startled was O'Phelan that he brought up his trembling hands to try to stop the flow of wine into his lap.

Flushed with pleasure at the success of his colourful uncapping, the fevered Bagenal spun the other pistol in his right hand and aimed it at the hesitant partakers. It came to rest on the tutor.

'Come on now, my fellow, drink up,' he roared at the shaking tutor. O'Phelan was hypnotized by the red stains on his fawn-coloured trousers. He made no sound, he could not move, indeed, he did not see the pistol aimed at his ear until the Member of Parliament tucked the point of the barrel playfully into his neck. Terrified, the tutor screamed, and stood up so quickly that glasses and plates scattered around him to the floor. He ran to the door, knocking into two footmen as he careened past them. Laughter at the table, led by the tutor's pupil, Eleanor, was raucous. The M.P. restored his pistols to their case and fell back into his chair, delighted by his success, downed a full goblet of claret, and promptly joined Lord Butler in sleep, his head resting on the table on the edge of the claret pool. No one paid any attention, so intent were the still-awake guests to hear Lady Eleanor's detailed philippic against her tutor's unseemly cowardice, womanly nerves, and general ineptitude.

The next morning Theo O'Phelan was gone, having packed his clothes and books and set out on foot to Kilkenny to join the stagecoach to Dublin before the household was awake.

An elegant, grey Georgian house called Woodstock stands on a hill facing towards the town of Inistiogue twelve miles distant. It 'commands the village,' Sir William Fownes, the Squire, says, when the name of the house is mentioned. The grounds on every side are well kept, ringed by an ancient planting of great oaks. Scattered here and there among them, unclothed statues of Greek maidens hug their marble flesh against the Irish damp. Thick woods beyond the oaks and yews shelter pied goats who periodically make themselves useful in the sunny patches of the day by cropping the lawns. In places where the goats have been left too long, the grass is yellow and limp, fogged over and full of sprets. Far back of the house the grass grows full and heavy, surrounded and laced with arbutus in which a muster of Lady Betty Fownes' peacocks stalk periodically.

The house appears to sit firmly, settled and perfectly balanced like a steamer on calm seas. The stolid effect is due to the precise arrangement of windows—eight on each floor symmetrically arranged around and above the great central door. In the late afternoon the windows turn a many-eyed vision upon the driveway that curves up to, and then away from, the door. At sunset, on a day that has been sunny, the windows seem to become overly bright and then blind and incapable any longer of spying on hopeful arrivals or disgruntled departures.

The ordeal of the long morning and somnolent afternoon is almost over. Sarah Ponsonby sits on a stone bench, mercifully, she thinks, hidden from the eyes of the house by the high box hedge that surrounds what Lady Betty calls her 'improved' garden. Sarah's eyes are on a copy of *Clarissa*, but she is not reading. She passes over the lines of close print with no effort at comprehension, trying to establish the fact of her total absorption in the novel for anyone, especially Sir William, should he chance to come upon her.

It has been a trying day. The weariness Sarah feels stems from the number of moves she has been compelled to make to keep herself out of her uncle's path and to avoid Lady Betty's sad eyes. It is not easy. From the time of Sir William's early morning trip to the village to his return, there is a safe respite. Then, close to the time for his supper, he rushes in muddy boots through the halls to his office at the rear of the house. When Sarah is foolish enough to remain indoors, or when the weather is too unpleasant to allow her the haven of the gardens, she will hear him at her door, knocking, sometimes pounding. She remains very still and does not respond to his angry 'Come on now, girl, open up!' When she remains silent, he leaves, swearing. At his office, ill-tempered and impatient, he receives the petitions of his tenants and his manager's many complaints about the tenants. Today, from her stone bench, Sarah hears his horse's hoofbeats and surmises he has come home early for some reason. From that moment she begins to plan her desperate strategy of hide-and-be-sought among the bushes, behind the curved hedges, in the high places that shield the kitchen garden from the stables, but not, if she can manage it, in her room, where she fears she may be trapped by his unavoidable bulk and rude demands.

From where she sits, Sarah can see the chimneys and the upper windows of Woodstock. She regards the strict orderliness of its architecture, the carefully balanced progresses of the paths, gardens, and hedges as deceptive, outward denials of the inner chaos of her home. She knows the lives within are permeated with passion, suppressed anger, explosive language. Her own spirit has always been fearful and depressed, an orphan presence among highborn kinfolk who are obliged to keep her. The resentment they must feel, she believes, may be seen in Lady Betty's cool uncaring. In her aunt's pointed withdrawal from her, Sarah recognizes a repetition of her own mother's willful desertion of her by death when Sarah was four. And Sir William: his frightening spurts of aggressive energy against her are surely signs that he regards her presence in his house as intrusive. There are viscounts and major generals in the Fownes and Ponsonby lineage, of whom Sarah Ponsonby is quietly proud, and so she is familiar with the alliance between high birth, gout, and bad temper. But she cannot understand Sir William's red-faced accosting of her in places where, despite all her strategies, he finds her alone. What can she make of the terrible bloodshot fury in his eyes, the oppression of his great stomach pushed against her, his heavy hands imprisoning hers against a brick wall, or the crimson wainscoting, or a prickly hedge?

She thinks she hears him now, walking back and forth over the pebbles of the walk near her seat, back and forth, as though he is unable to settle upon a direction. Can he be reviewing the harsh words in her note delivered to him this morning upon his departure for the village by her maid Mary-Caryll? Is he deciding upon the shape of his answer, his revenge?

Then he came upon her, his feet trodding down the delicate weeds in the pathway, dislocating settled pebbles. He sat beside her, pushing her to the edge of the bench and then pulling her to him. Her book fell to the ground. With a rough slash, he pushed down her pelisse and dug with his fat fingers into her breast. The blue veins in his neck rose like a tangle of angered snakes: the brocade of her dress protested under his tugs. His swollen legs and feet pained him even as he caressed her: he muttered about the pain and tried to rest his leg on her lap. She pushed his old leg away. Old? Yes. She had heard he is about to celebrate his fiftieth birthday. The closely planted beech trees beyond the hedge leaned in protectively, trying to shield her, save her, from him. Perhaps, in their compassionate zeal, they will bend too far and fall in upon them, their soft foliage separating her from her hateful uncle. Yes, here they came. He was startled by the intrusion, fearing a branch would land across his gouted feet and gross legs, pinning him forever to the stone bench. But she was relieved, saved. She parted the beneficent leaves gently and started up from the bench, the charitable beeches holding him long enough for her to make her escape and disappear. She believed the trees had effected her revenge upon Sir William (he who was to her more goat than 'most honourable man,' a designation her aunt always gave him), cementing him for all eternity to the cold stone until his legs petrified.

Sunk into her vision, Sarah waits to be discovered by her uncle. 'He now has my letter. He must be very angry with me,' she tells herself. She is confused by his seeming presence beside her a moment ago and now his absence. She does not understand why, of all afternoons, this day he chooses to exempt her from his attentions. She picks up *Clarissa*, finds her place in its pages and continues to stare at the same lines. Her relief at being alone is short-lived. Shadows cross the long lengths of the lawn; she stands up to see card tables being laid under the trees nearest the house. Dinner is to be served there, as it often is on warm afternoons. She must make her way to it, to Mary-Caryll's kind but unspoken sympathy at her increasing peril, to Lady Betty's suffering reserve, to Sir William, his wig slipped down over his perspiring forehead to his eyebrows, his leg resting on a chair, his eyes in hot pursuit of her.

Their daily lives are composed of small scandals. Women, always only women, come to call. Sometimes, they arrive just after luncheon, in time to be invited to ceremonial cake and tea. They talk in low voices above noises of spoons and forks on china. Sarah cuts squares of quince cake and offers the plates. This day, mother, daughters, grand-aunts, and grandmother of the Wigman family come to report little discoveries while they are still fresh in their minds. Their coach has come directly from a visit to Kilbride, and before that to Dublin. They come freshly provided with tempting little tidbits for quick consumption. Today, they have brought word of the Warden's youngest daughter, who, they've just learned, at fifteen is sent to the old nursery for her meals because she has grown so excessively fat at her middle. Can it be? . . . No, they agree, of course it must mean that she is being kept from temptation at the family table.

Annoyed at not having succeeded in making his escape before the ladies' arrival, Sir William stands in the corner draining his teacup. He harrumphs, coughs, and then rolls phlegm around in his mouth, his cheeks puffed out. He sends a brown stream into the corner of the room. He looks at Sarah and smiles, his stippled nose pointed towards her chest, his eyes very small, bright, hungry. Sarah turns away in her chair to watch Lady Betty refill the cups, feeling Sir William's eyes on her back. Suddenly she seems to lose the balance between her hands, and her piece of quince cake slides to the floor. Mary-Caryll crosses the room from the corner where she has been wiping up the Squire's expectoration and sweeps up the crumbles of cake in her hands. Her fingers are stained brown, Sarah sees, when Mary-Caryll places a fresh piece of cake on her plate. Grand-aunt Mrs Wigman narrates the scandalous behaviour of the Warden's parlour maid, who failed to return home until midnight from a dance at Inistiogue. When she finally appeared, she was without her hat or shoes, losses she insisted were due to a high wind.

Sarah feels queasy. She thinks her stays are too tight. Before her eyes she sees Mary-Caryll's stained fingers restoring the cake. She excuses herself, goes quickly into the garden, and is sick into the broken fountain. She covers her vomit with leaves, wipes her forehead and chin with her petticoat, goes in at the back kitchen entry and up the stairs to her room. She tells herself she must remember to tell the gardener about the fountain.

Sarah Ponsonby could recall only a vague, foglike sense of loss when her own mother died, exhausted by Chambré Brabazon Ponsonby's abnormal jealousy of his beautiful young second wife and by the terrible isolation in which he had incarcerated her. Sarah was four. Three years later her father died when his horse failed to stop at a barn and crushed him against the closed half-door at the top.

All she was ever able to remember about her father was a story he had told her of his father, Henry Ponsonby, a general at the Battle of Flanders and then, at Dettingen. In 1745, her grandfather and his company were stationed high on a hill between the enemy-infested Barry Woods and the fortified town of Fontenoy. Sarah's father, Chambré, was the general's aide-de-camp, still almost a boy, whose service to his father was not unlike that of a body valet. During a furious exchange of gunfire, the general handed his son his watch and ring, for what reason Chambré was never afterwards able to ascertain: was it because he felt more capable of loading his musket without the burden of timepiece and signet? Or had he been granted a curious foreknowledge and so entrusted his belongings to his son for safekeeping? Chambré lay down to avoid the too-close-for-comfort cannon balls tearing through the air from the direction of the Woods. His father paused to take from his pocket his enameled box and insert into each nostril a pinch of snuff. As he returned the box to his pocket, his head was blown off and away, at such a distance and in such condition that his shocked son could not retrieve it.

Sarah was orphaned and left to the mercies of her stepmother and a nastily playful stepbrother who enjoyed tying the little girl to trees or fenceposts in the course of the outlaw games he devised. Her stepmother referred to her, in company, as 'a slattern of a girl.' When her stepmother was carried off by a sudden, lethal infection brought on by quaffing, by herself, what she called 'a sober quart of claret,' the twelve-year-old girl felt nothing but relief. Sarah was an earnest, slight, pretty, often sad girl, closer to womanhood than her years would suggest. She had lived a life of practised self-protection against her family and against the Fates. At her stepmother's funeral, Sarah, who had little experience in arranging her life, who was indeed too sensitive and retiring, too often melancholic and silent, to try, who had drifted from the care of one uncaring adult to the next, spoke shyly to her Aunt Betty Fownes, her own mother's somewhat elderly cousin, inquiring if it were possible there might be a place for her to live at Woodstock. Lady Betty's sweet, placid face dissolved in sympathy for the homelessness of the young orphan. Her own daughter being married and gone away at some distance, the kindly matron agreed at once that there was indeed room for her. She would be pleased, she said, for Sarah's company.

So it was that Sarah came to live with Lady Betty and fat, proud, lascivious, gouted Sir William Fownes, who hoped, in his heartless way, to convince his wife of her terminal ill health in order to free him for another marriage. To her every symptom (and she was troubled by many), he attributed a terrible affliction that he considered might materialize, with persuasion and iteration, into something mortal.

Lady Betty, on the other hand, was only too well acquainted with her husband's weaknesses. She understood his unsavoury ambition for her, and was grateful that gout prevented him from serious pursuit of chambermaids, pub girls, and (for shame, she recalled) their own daughter, Julia, who had escaped her father's attentions by marrying Harry Tighe when she was fifteen and moving to Kilbride. If Lady Betty was distant with Sarah it was not out of unkindness, for she loved her cousin's daughter and was strongly engrained with family feeling, but for fear that any special notice of her niece would cause Sir William to become aware of her growing beauty.

Lady Betty was a good woman, so good that the story told about her at teas and suppers in the County was this:

There lurked along the wet, rutted, sometimes impassable Kilkenny county roads, a robber named Freyney, a native of Inistiogue, who had been a servant at Woodstock until Sir William dismissed him for insubordination. Freyney's huge black head, giant body, grasping hands, and loaded musket terrified passersby whom he robbed but then allowed to go on unharmed. Sir William had been held up by Freyney a number of times, even when he was accompanied by armed retainers who turned out to be too slow for the skilled highwayman. In fact, Freyney appeared to be especially vindictive about the Squire of Woodstock. It was learned later that Freyney's favourite uncle had worked on the restoration of the Fownes's house, Winter Lodge, near Dublin, investing in his work two years of fine carpentry and many costly materials. Upon its completion, and before he had paid the luckless uncle, Sir William sold the house at good profit, transferring his debt to the new proprietor, who promptly disowned it. The uncle was ruined and died soon after, having bled to death from a saw cut on his wrist. His nephew vowed to avenge his death, and did so, periodically, each time he pushed Sir William into a muddy ditch after relieving him of his purse and his travelling breeches.

But Lady Betty (she is the heroine of this widely told tale) passed on the same dangerous roads without accident. Freyney, it was said, would spot her coach or would be informed about its approach in advance by friends on the household staff, the same informants who kept him apprised of Sir William's movements. So great was his respect for her, perhaps for her well-known suffering under Sir William's callous treatment, that he lay down in a ditch beside the road to allow Lady Betty to pass unalarmed even by the sight of him.

Lady Betty decided that it might be wise to send Sarah away to school, less to provide her with an education (for girls required very little of that to occupy a worthy place in Irish society) than to insure the pretty young girl's safety from Sir William's wandering eye. Miss Parke's Academy for Young Ladies in Kilkenny was chosen for the thirteen-year-old Sarah more for its location, twenty-five miles from Woodstock, and its cost, twelve guineas the year, than for its reputation for learning. Sarah was sent off in a coach accompanied by Lady Betty rather than Sir William, guaranteeing her safe passage on the hazardous roads north.

The school in 1768 (it was to last only ten more years and then decline for lack of funds into a less pretentious working-girls' place for instruction in lace making) was housed in a dingy, stiff, spiritless town building. The instructions mistress, Miss Parke herself, a vinegary spinster, believed in teaching domestic and practical arts. No time was wasted on studies that might culminate in dangerous ideas or independent thought. Her pupils, fourteen young girls of good families, were taught to do fine embroidery and make neat, if somewhat inaccurate, maps of the County, the country, the British Isles, and even the continent to which it was thought they were sure to travel some day. The girls were also instructed in the rudiments of the French language (to serve the same ultimate purpose as the maps) and trained to have an elegant, elaborate, spidery hand. Whist playing was offered; it was elected by everyone and practised assiduously by the girls in the evenings for halfpenny the point. There was a good cook attached to the school but no chamber help, so the girls did their own 'besom-business,' as they privately called it, sweeping dust balls from beneath one bed to the next.

At Miss Parke's, Sarah was lonely and isolated. She quickly became proficient at the ladylike labours assigned to her and played a good hand at cards, but she made no real friends among her twittery, featherheaded classmates, who thought her too serious and always very sad.

Lady Betty made one kindly provision for the girl in her exile. She wrote to Mrs Adelaide Butler of Kilkenny Castle (whom she had known in Dublin in her girlhood) and told her of her niece's stay nearby, expressing the hope that it might be possible for little Sarah to visit the Butlers, perhaps during one of the school holidays, because (this she did not add) she feared the girl's return to the dangers of Woodstock. Inadvertently, Lady Betty almost ruined the prospective invitation for Sarah by addressing her old acquaintance as Mrs Walter Butler rather than by her assumed title. Lady Adelaide chose to overlook this country ignorance and invited Sarah to spend the two weeks surrounding Easter at Kilkenny Castle.

*   *   *

Sarah in her best dress and bonnet sat sedately in the uncomfortable fiddle-backed chair Milligan had pointed her to. Then he said:

'Lady Butler asked would you be good enough to wait here. Her daughter will be with you directly.'

Sarah waited. She inspected the austere browning portraits, assuming that the persons seated stiffly in them must be dukes of Ormonde. She studied the inhospitable French chairs with Orpheus harps built into their backs that were dwarfed by the immense size of the drawing room, the tapestries into which dogs of uncertain breed and grey mythical animals had been woven among beds of vague flowers and the remains of grottoes.

No one came. Sarah walked to the long windows opening upon a stone porch and a military-looking parapet. Beyond was a great meadowlike area bordered by cherry trees. She watched a sturdy man come quickly through a path in the tall grass and approach the house. It must be Mr Walter Butler, she thought, noting how determinedly, surefootedly, his booted legs cut through the grass. As he came closer she saw a head of short red curls and what appeared to be a knife-sharp nose and pointed chin. Not Mr Butler, clearly: a son? or younger brother?

She returned to her assigned chair to await his arrival. Anything is better than a return to Miss Parke's deserted halls, she thought. The young man's footsteps could be heard on the porch, the doors opened. A setter puppy ran across the carpet and put his muddy front paws on Sarah's dress, my *only* company dress, she thought.

'O dear,' she said, and tried to push him down.

'I *am* sorry,' said the young man, who had entered

immediately behind the ebullient dog. 'Here, let me take her. Down, Lento.' He reached to Sarah's lap, scooped up the wriggling dog, and strode with him to the door, which he closed quickly behind him, and returned, pulling a chair to Sarah's side.

'Rude of me to be so late. Please excuse me.' The young man had a pleasantly low voice and an open, free manner that seemed to Sarah to sound unusually sincere.

'Not at all. I've enjoyed looking about. I'm Sarah Ponsonby. Mrs Butler was good enough to invite me to visit during the recess of my school.'

'Yes, of course, I know all about you. You're very welcome. I'm Eleanor Butler, Lady Adelaide's daughter.'

Their friendship grew rapidly. Sarah adjusted to the transformation of the young man become Lady Eleanor. Eleanor was delighted to have a ready companion for her outdoor life. Sarah shared her pleasure. On rain-soaked afternoons, just before the descent of dusk, when they felt incarcerated too long in the castle, they walked through back paths, as far from the house as they could progress without leaving the desmesne. Eleanor often went a little ahead, her booted feet covering the rough places more securely than Sarah's more decorous steps. On overcast days, when the chairs they had occupied all day seemed hard and the confines of their rooms oppressive, they set out for what Eleanor called a ramble. She told Sarah she wanted to show her the north end of the property.

'Here we try to grow fruit trees. The trees grow well enough, I suppose, but we have little success with the fruit. What the birds do not expropriate, the tenants' boys filch at night,' Eleanor said.

Sarah smiled and shook her head, indicating whole-hearted disapproval of such natural and unnatural assaults upon the property of the gentry. Her steps were prim and careful, for she was afraid she would stumble over the cobbles and look foolish to Eleanor's cool eyes. Once, her ankle turned, but before she fell, Eleanor was at her side, her strong hands supporting her. Sarah was startled, feeling much as she once had when Sir William had appeared without warning on a garden path at Woodstock.

Another day, a grey, mooning donkey thrust his furry head at them out of a hedgerow. The suddenness of the animal's appearance moved the Ladies close together in an act of mutual protection. They collided, Sarah uttered a small 'oh.' Eleanor said nothing but made no move away from Sarah. Now they proceeded, their shoulders, their hands occasionally coming together. When they encountered rough places in the walk, Eleanor's guiding hand was at Sarah's elbow. Slowly Sarah learned not to be surprised by Eleanor's abrupt and lordly manner, and to recognize beneath her rough gestures a companion hungry, as was Sarah herself, for the touch of friendship and the unexpected warmth of closeness.

When unbending sheets of rain came down too hard to allow them to leave the house, they sat before the fire in Eleanor's sitting room. Eleanor read aloud from her elegantly bound translation of Plutarch's *Lives*, and Sarah listened, intent on understanding the difficult prose. Eleanor read to her about Gaius, whose oratorical voice was so extravagantly high that his friend would play upon his pitch pipe to bring the sound down to a proper level. Sarah felt outside the bounds of Eleanor's formidable learning. Eleanor must have sensed this: she put her book down, went over to Sarah's chair, and put her hand gently on her shoulder.

'Does all this heavy biography bore you?' she asked.

'No, not bore me. Frighten me, because there is so much for me to learn, and Miss Parke's school teaches us nothing of Latin and Greek personages. I've never heard of Hadrian. Are you shocked at that?'

'No, I am not shocked. I would enjoy teaching you. Very much.' Eleanor's hand hovered over Sarah's hair. Sarah looked up into her eyes, waiting, wondering what this kindness, this little approach, this almost-caress could signify. Confused herself about her own intention, Eleanor lowered her arm and went back to her chair at the other side of the hearth.

'Very much,' she said, and Sarah, filled with a rush of pleasure she had not expected, said:

'I would like that very much.'

After a fortnight of walking the grounds and exploring the nearby town, reading and listening, talking before the fire and in their beds, smiling at each other surreptitiously across the silent supper table and laughing together during their private breakfasts at the prospect of spending the day ahead alone together, Sarah knew she loved Eleanor. It was an unbidden and only half-understood passion, compounded of the accumulated, unused affection of her thirteen loveless years. Trusting in the extraordinary reality of her feelings, she now took Eleanor's hand when they walked.

'In case a donkey appears without warning,' she told Eleanor and smiled, pretending that a threat to her security was required to explain her action.

37

Before they retired to their beds, Sarah allowed herself to be kissed gently, an act Eleanor initiated as though it was a parallel to Sarah's reaching for her hand. Sarah then returned the kiss, as gently.

A silent pact had been consummated, an unspoken statement was broadcast from the two women to the brocaded chairs and hangings, to the gardens and stone lions of Eleanor's childhood. Connected thus, they moved everywhere together, saying very little now to each other that was personal, afraid of declarative words and phrases, trusting the annealing power of touch and glance. Sarah was in awe of the alchemy that had translated Eleanor's mannish angularity into the womanliness of her soft caresses. Now Sarah knew: Under the mannerliness and solicitude of a young man there dwelled the warmth and concern of a woman.

Near the end of Sarah's stay, they took a last walk to the elms at the edge of the park. Eleanor moved a few steps off the path to show Sarah a vista through the trees; Sarah followed obediently. There, clearly too surprised by their human presence to move, were two small foxes, their pearly eyes glittering in the early evening moonlight, their severe, pointed noses raised into the air as if they scorned the scent of the two women.

'Don't move,' warned Eleanor, putting her arm across Sarah's chest to keep her from stepping forward.

'I'm not afraid,' said Sarah.

'Perhaps not. But they are.' Eleanor's voice was rough, almost angry. An opportunity to protect Sarah from danger had been denied her, and she could not hide her dis-

38

appointment. The foxes moved away, their retreating tails grey plumes in the dark brush.

'Do you think they saw us?' Sarah whispered.

'Of course. They say foxes see very well in the dark.'

Eleanor gathered her dusty skirts in one hand and took Sarah's hand with the other. Sarah's fingers felt crushed in Eleanor's heavy gloves but she made no move to remove her hand, thinking that Eleanor might interpret this as rejection.

In their rooms, on the last evening of the holiday, Eleanor threw three giant logs on the fire, creating a rush of flame and smoke in the mammoth opening above the hearth. Sarah shrank back as from a blow, backing into Eleanor, who stood behind her watching the conflagration, pleased with the enormity of her creation.

'Oh dear . . .'

'It's fine. Don't move.'

Then they laughed together, comfortably, communally, remembering the encounter with the foxes when Sarah froze at Eleanor's command into absolute attention. Now Eleanor's arms were around Sarah's shoulders, as if she were presenting her to the great fire, as if she were offering her for immolation by some devouring fire god. Sarah slipped down through them to the floor. Eleanor lowered herself. One behind the other, they stared at the fire, aware of each other's breathing and heart beat. Sarah turned to touch Eleanor's cheek, needing to be reassured of her warm presence.

Eleanor never doubted, from the moment she looked into Sarah's eyes, as deep blue as speedwells, and saw her pale slight face and pure sweet mouth, her brows as black and straight as calligraphic dashes, her childlike frame and straight, inky black hair, that, at long last, she had uncovered the mystery behind her own confused emotional life. Now she understood the meaning of the quirky enigmas of her dreams, the fantasies of her girlhood rides on the stone lions. Now knowing for what she had been waiting during her thirty-four empty years, she recognized in Sarah the missing object of her heart. Never again, she vowed to herself, would she be willing to be parted from her.

For five years letters, notes, cameos, woven locks of hair encased in lockets, keepsakes, and inscribed books passed between Sarah Ponsonby and Eleanor Butler. On holiday, Sarah often came to the castle. In the long months between they wrote daily or, on rare occasion, Eleanor would travel in the marketing chaise and have it leave her and her basket at Miss Parke's gate. There she announced herself as Lady Eleanor Butler to see Miss Sarah Ponsonby with messages from home, like a lady bountiful come with provisions to a needy tenant.

Lady Adelaide knew of Eleanor's fondness for the schoolgirl and considered it salutory.

'She is good for our Eleanor. When they are together Eleanor is less moody and irritable,' she told His Lordship, who grunted his indifference to Eleanor's moods, and added more claret to his glass. Lady Betty, when she heard of the visits and the accounts of Sarah's contented stays at the castle, was glad that her niece was occupied happily, away from Woodstock, pleased that Sarah was being opened to the ways of aristocratic life and manners.

Sarah and Eleanor's letters to each other were full of an urgency, a longing unknown to the families:

June 1774: 'Believe me, my dearest friend, I would come if I could, I will come when I can. My wrenched knee now keeps me in, and makes visits difficult. My company is Lento, who has lost all his wild ways and become a sedate dog, and my thoughts of you. I am unhappy at home, but I cannot always persuade my parents, even when my knee is healed, of my need of the carriage to travel to market to assuage my moods. I suspect they are all too aware that you are the destination I seek.'

September 1774: 'My dearest love, I remember as I close my eyes at night how fine you looked in the night shirt I embroidered for you, how it fit your wonderful shoulders and fell to your ankles exactly as I had planned. Miss Parke thought me very diplomatic and gracious to have spent so much time on linen for Lord Butler. I made no effort to correct her mistaken notion.'

March 1775: 'How delightful that we shall have the whole time from Palm Sunday to Maundy Thursday alone in our rooms! Will your parents return that evening or early Good Friday? I must know quickly because I am making a large card with the days, even the hours, embossed upon it in Gothic with deep blue, almost indigo ink. As the days pass I encircle them with green. I want to make a duplicate for you. Or is it foolish me alone who tracks the time so longingly while I practise my handwriting under Miss Parke's eye? She does not know what to make of my choice of exercise subjects.'

May 1778: 'I am told I must leave school at month's end and return permanently to Woodstock. My friends have assisted me in placing my clothes and books, my embroidery frames and pens and ink, in wicker boxes. Uncle William is sending the carriage and pair. The vest I have embroidered with gold and purple thread for you will be delivered to the castle by Mary Elton-

Casey who passes on her way to her home. I w^d, if I c^d, be passing y^r way too, rather than travelling to Woodstock. I w^d have no wish to return home except for Frisk, who misses me and is said to howl at night for loneliness. I shall be in exile from you. Soon after I arrive, you will have word from me. I hope you will reply quickly, O my love.'

When Eleanor wrote to Woodstock it was to reassure Sarah that somehow a way would be found for them to be together. The distance between them was now great, twenty-five miles on a road often rendered impassable or dangerous by rain, mud, robbers. At first they sent each other daily letters to keep up their spirits.

Sarah wrote: 'Woodstock is beautiful now. Frisk and I walk about much of the day, accompanied by a book in which I read while I rest. The gardens are especially fine, the pond full of small leaping fish that glitter in the sun as they rise and fall, almost in one motion. Now and then I catch sight of our stand of partridge. At dusk I often walk in the formal higher grounds. The perfection of this spring makes me sad: w^d that you were here with me.'

Eleanor responded in a burst of hopeful prose designed to hearten Sarah: 'Not too much longer, my beloved, before we will find a way to be united. As soon as I can devise a plan that will persuade them over the natural objections that will be made against what is in our minds and hearts to effect.'

Sarah had been home almost a year—eleven months and twenty-one days, according to the elegantly embroidered calendar she made and kept secretly in her clothes press—

when she came to the end of her endurance of Sir William. At first, she shielded Eleanor from knowledge of her uncle's sly pursuit of her, feeling that generalisations about her unhappiness would better serve her friend's hot temper and peace of mind, but she could no longer disguise her true feelings.

She wrote: 'At first I believed it was impossible for so professed a man of honour to throw off his mask so shamefully. I thought if I were prudent I would be secured from appearing to understand his intentions towards me. Believe me, dear beloved, this was my hope, vain now, as I know. To whom can I turn? I must spare poor Lady Betty. Neither my pride, my resentment, nor any other passion shall ever be sufficiently powerful to make me give her any uneasiness, any suspicion of the true state of affairs between her husband and me. Unhappy as I am, I sometimes laugh to think of the earnestness with which she presses me to be obliging to him. How terrible it all is. My love, help me.'

Eleanor's shock could be heard in the reply she returned early the next day: 'Try to avoid his presence, my dearest, until I can rescue you. You must be quick, you must be clever, above all, you must be careful. Now I know there is no time to be lost in my plans. You must think always of yourself, as do I, and of me, so that you do not stumble into his path.'

Sarah's most poignant letter was sent not to Eleanor but to Sir William, in his own house. She hoped thereby to rid herself of the pain of her suspicions, to be free of his attentions, to accost him with a letter, because she so feared a personal encounter.

Her letter, in beautiful script that she entrusted to Mary-Caryll to deliver, was this: 'I desire to be informed in writing, and only in writing, whether your motive for behaving as you do towards me is a desire that I should quit your house. If so, I promise in the most solemn manner that I shall take the first opportunity of doing so, and that my real motive for leaving shall ever be concealed from my dear Lady Betty, and from the world. Sarah.'

To Eleanor she sent a copy of this letter. Nothing she might have done could have made her situation so clearly desperate.

Eleanor was aghast. From Sir William came no response. Sarah watched him anxiously at table, at their brief encounters in halls and on landings. When their eyes met his seemed blank and uncomprehending, as though he had received no communication from her or had misplaced it before he had time to read it. For three days Sarah waited for a reply. The writing that came to her, by messenger, was from the castle in Eleanor's close-lettered, crabbed script: 'I shall come Friday night next. We will meet in the old Chippery barn. At close to ten, if I do not fall off the horse. I will bring my love, my love.'

Mary-Caryll had served in the Fownes household since her dismissal from Sheepshead Inn at Inistiogue, where she both tended to the bar and kept the peace. She was a woman built like an oak tree, almost thirteen stone, and three inches more than six feet tall. During an altercation at closing time one night she threw a lethal candlestick at an unruly patron who had reached into the dress of a young barmaid and then been told to leave by Molly, the Bruiser, as Mary-Caryll was called in the pub. After the funeral she appealed to Sir William and was given a chambermaid's berth at Woodstock: Lady Betty was touched by the towering woman's quick defense of virtue.

Mary-Caryll had no family, so her move to Woodstock was easily accomplished. Her arms were as broad and strong as a ploughman's. Her chambermaid's duties seemed too light, too easy to her. But she went about them willingly and was especially devoted to the care of the person and room of small, quiet Sarah Ponsonby, whose plight in the house she sensed was not unlike that of the barmaid she had so staunchly defended. Her fidelities had always been simple, direct, and on behalf of the weak: a deserted cat, her overworked mother, who died in her arms after a fire that destroyed their cottage, the homeless thirteen-year-old barmaid who slept on a shelf behind the bar of the Sheepshead Inn, and now the orphaned and threatened Miss Ponsonby.

It was a cold wet evening early in April in the year 1778, in the same year that British soldiers in another hemisphere began to taste the bitter food of foreign defeat. Sarah Ponsonby said goodbye to Mary-Caryll, pressed upon her a small purse of coins, and then stepped out of a downstairs window into a flower bed. Mary-Caryll handed out Sarah's portmanteau and basket containing Frisk, his muzzle bound up with a silk scarf. They whispered farewell, waved; Sarah put frisk under one arm, her bag in her hand, and set off in the half light down the road towards Waterford.

It was a hazardous way of departure, but Sarah feared the giveaway noises of the great front door and preferred to risk a twisted ankle. Outside the high hawthorn hedge, she met a labourer with a lantern whom Mary-Caryll had hired. He relieved her of her portmanteau. Together they set out to cover the three miles south to the old barn, deserted since the Chippery family had moved to Tipperary to try their fortunes with sheep. A thin steady rain fell. By the time they reached the place, Sarah's cape was sodden. The rain had run down her neck to soak the worsted shirt Mary-Caryll had removed without permission from a houseman's trunk. Her long skirt, one of Mary-Caryll's own, was in danger of falling down, so wet was it, so insufficient the cord belt Mary-Caryll had devised. The labourer held the door open for her. She gave him a gold piece and thanked him for his services, and he went on his way to his home near Thomastown.

Eleanor was not there. Sarah huddled in a corner and lit the candle Mary-Caryll had wisely sent with her. She took out the loaded pistol obtained by the provident maid from Sir William's study and placed it beside her. She took off her wet cap, another Mary-Caryll borrowing that covered her hair, but she was too cold, too weary to remove her wet cape. She lay back against the truss of old, acrid hay, hoping it would absorb some of the moisture. Was Eleanor waylaid? Had she fallen as she rode? Had she been prevented from leaving the castle? Where *was* she? Would she come at all? Sarah's fears and doubts multiplied. She clung to her little dog though his frail, furless body offered small protection. The sounds overhead, and beyond the barn door, were strange to her. They rang with menace: retainers of Sir William? A band of curious and hungry foxes? Owls? Robbers?

Where was Eleanor? Tired by waiting, huddled with Frisk against the cold, Sarah dozed and did not hear hoofbeats approaching. But she started up at the sound of the barn door pushed aside. The candle went out. In the small light of the quarter moon she thought she saw the outline of a man. She screamed, stood up, and grabbed the pistol.

'Don't be frightened, my love. It is I, Eleanor. For the love of God, don't shoot me.'

Sarah fell to her knees before Eleanor, sobbing. Eleanor knelt down and took her in her arms. They clung to each other, Sarah shaking from fright, relief, and chill, Eleanor attempting to calm and warm her.

'We'll stay the night here and wait for morning to see if the road is clear,' Eleanor told Sarah. She relit the candle and went to find her horse. He munched happily on the hay she provided and then she tethered him in a dry corner of the barn. She latched the barn door and lay down beside Sarah. They put their arms about each other, ignoring the wet discomforts of their clothes, seeking to dry themselves in the heat of their creature love. Sarah shook with chill, Eleanor's nerves quivered, but to Sarah she appeared to be a tower of calm, a secure, comforting, and warm presence, a gallant rescuer from all peril, a goddess of love and safety. For hours they could not sleep. The rough men's clothes rubbed their backs and arms against the hay mattress. Like orphaned strays, like fairy-tale children, they lay together and slept at last in the first light of dawn, two runaway women of quality in an abandoned barn, escaped from the protection of great houses and powerful men into a singular enterprise.

While they slept well into the morning, Lord Butler's searchers passed the Chippery barn on their way to Waterford to find the missing Lady Eleanor. At noon a chaise rolled past the barn in the same direction, bearing messengers of the distressed Lady Betty in search of the missing niece whose dog and clothes were gone, and whose bed had not been slept in.

Lord Butler arrived at Woodstock in the early afternoon to inquire if Lady Eleanor was there.

'She is not,' said a disturbed Sir William, who had consoled himself with a number of black-cherry whiskeys. His perturbation was great, for he feared that the escaped Sarah would not remember the promise of discretion in her letter to him.

'And what is more, our Sarah is gone off.'

Lord Butler was not concerned. 'Lord Kilbriggin has been hanging about her,' he said, more to himself than to Sir William. 'It must be him. They've run off together. That bastard cur . . .'

'But . . .'

'There is nothing to do but send to Dublin and to Waterford.' Lord Butler was in his carriage before Sir William could say anything more.

To the families it was inconceivable that Sarah and Eleanor had absconded—Sir William's word for Sarah's act. How? Why? Where to? The answers to questions about the extraordinary event awaited the results of the chase. While men rode about the countryside, searching everywhere for the runaways, Eleanor and Sarah slept on in the windowless, freezing barn, Eleanor sunk in dreamless content, Sarah engulfed by dreams of riderless horses, soft-breasted flower beds, nights of mud and blackness, great bellies encased in brocade, tea-stained spittle. She roamed the paths of Woodstock pursued by furred black and white owls that dove at her head and grabbed at her hair with yellow claws. The women woke in the afternoon in each other's arms, at first exultant at the extraordinary fortune that had brought them so far to this unlikely union.

Sarah was breathing heavily. She was feverish and still weary after their long sleep. Eleanor decided they must remain in the barn another day and night to allow Sarah's illness to subside. Sarah felt too sick to protest. While she slept, Eleanor watched and worried about their future. How would they live on the little they had brought with them? Would their families relent and send them support once they had removed themselves from Irish scandal? Would society in England, or Wales, or Scotland, or wherever they could find lodgings, *have* them, accept them as they wished to be: two loving women *married* in each other's eyes, determined without the shadow of a doubt to live with no one except each other for the rest of their lives?

In the morning Sarah was still sluggish and hot. Eleanor sent her horse back along the road to Kilkenny, trusting his instinct to find his master. They moved on, walking quickly through the market towns of Kilmacow and Mullinavat. They climbed over the mountain into Inistiogue, where they paused only to rent a hackney carriage to take them on to Waterford. Settled into it, they talked gently of money, destination, the often stormy passage to Milford Haven, the hope of baths and clean clothes in Waterford. Frisk slept beside them in his basket.

Lady Betty wrote to her daughter Julia: 'I am in utmost distress. My dear Sarah has leapt out of the window and is gone off. We surmise that Miss Butler of the castle is with her. Mr Butler had been to inquire for his daughter. He tells that Miss Butler left the castle just as the family went into supper and was not missed for three hours.'

They might have succeeded, had not Sarah, out of her head with fever, dropped her shirt ruffle as they left the barn. A searcher from the castle found it, thought it to be

Lady Eleanor's, and surmised from it the runaways' direction. Still it might have worked, they might have reached the harbour town of Waterford as they had planned, and made their escape by boat, had they not missed the English packet that travelled between Waterford and Milford Haven and been forced to wait for the next day in a room they rented for the night in an inn near the quai.

Eleanor ate her dinner alone in the back of the pub and brought up soup and fresh baker's bread to Sarah, who dozed, woke to drink a few mouthfuls of the broth, and slept again at once. Eleanor sat listening to her difficult breathing for some time, and then resolved: 'I must take her back. She is too sick for a journey over water. I am defeated, she is defeated, but not by the damnable Fownes and Butlers. We are defeated by this sickness. God help us now.'

A neighbour who had heard news of Sarah's disappearance (as who in the countryside had not by now?) sent a note to Lady Betty in the late afternoon: 'I pas't two Ladies in a Carr in men's clouths near W't'fd.' By then Lady Betty had left Woodstock to travel in that direction, passing the messenger bearing the note.

Mrs Tighe, whose memory of inconceivable girlhood events had been successfully buried, wrote to her mother: 'Of course I know well that more was imagin'd by y^r Sarah than was ever intended by my dear Father.'

Sarah woke, hot, and in tears. 'Oh love, what can I do?' As she spoke, Frisk barked and leaped onto the bed.

'Lie still. I have ordered a gig.'

'A *gig*? For Milford Haven?'

50

'No, my dearest. To take us back. Until you have recovered. Then we will come away again.'

'Oh no. No. Not back.'

'For a little while.'

'Do you think we have been missed?'

'I can't tell. Rest a bit yet.'

Almost at once, they knew the answer to Sarah's question. Led to the inn, and then the room, by the familiar high yipping of Sarah's greyhound, Lady Betty's manservant knocked on their door. Without waiting for a reply, he entered their room, calling over his shoulder: 'I have found them.' Sarah was in bed, Eleanor seated beside her, a basin of cool water in her lap, her hands filled with cloths. Startled by the intrusion, she overturned the basin, spilling water onto the bed, and stood up to shield Sarah from the sight of the manservant.

'Out, out,' she said, pushing at him with her strong hands, her face crimson with anger.

The man backed away, almost colliding with Lady Betty.

'Oh my dears, my dears,' she said when she saw the two women. Sarah started to cry at the sight of her aunt. Eleanor stood still, stony-faced, and made no effort to greet her.

Settled into the chaise, and awaiting the arrival of the driver, the three women were immobilised in front of the inn when Lord Butler's men, accompanied now by Morton Cavanaugh, Eleanor's brother-in-law, opened the door to their vehicle and demanded that Eleanor accompany them to Borris where the Cavanaughs had their house. Eleanor appealed to Lady Betty, who told the men Miss Eleanor, at her own request, was returning to Woodstock with them.

Sarah leaned back against the leather upholstery, too sick to make any protest, her eyes shut against what appeared in her fever to be a parade of unknown persons pushing and pulling each other in some wild tug-of-war game. No longer was she able to recognise anyone about her, including Eleanor and Lady Betty. Out of her head, she wandered in a world of black practices, covens preparing a broth of peacock eyes and red cocks to be sacrificed to a strange black man. A stick-thin witch named Alice Kyteler, dressed in her black devil's girdle and nothing else, her breasts resembling Eleanor's somehow, stirred a magic soup in the black skull of a criminal and then gave it to her. She served it to Sir William by pouring it slowly through a black hole in his monstrously swollen toe.

Eleanor refused to leave the carriage. Morton Cavanaugh and a manservant reached into it and pulled her out. Suddenly she lost the control that had steeled her throughout the dark ride on the black horse and the three dark days and nights. She screamed at the men that she wanted one half-hour alone with Sarah. But Lady Betty would not permit it, fearful of leaving her niece with the phrensied Eleanor. Left for a moment without the men's restraining hands, Eleanor climbed back into the carriage. Once more she was dragged out by her brother-in-law. Lady Betty bid Eleanor a tearful farewell, the driver mounted to his board, Eleanor was loaded into the Cavanaugh coach, and the two conveyances set off north, one behind the other, each bearing one of the runaway pair.

At Woodstock's gate Sarah awoke, undone by her sickness and her delirium. She thought Eleanor was beside her and cried out: 'My love, coven Alice Kyteler is to be flogged eight times for her cooking. We must save her,' and fell back unconscious.

* * *

Eleanor was now hysterical. The men held her arms behind her and pinned her to the seat as the coach bore them along the road to Borris.

Morton Cavanaugh wanted Eleanor to tell him the story of her sudden flight. When she was calm enough to speak, she would only say that their flight had *not* been sudden. For some time they had planned to go to England, to find a house and, for the rest of their lives, to live together. Cavanaugh made no reply to this madness. A burly, belligerent young man whose sweet, delicate wife Margaret leaned upon him for every need of her life and her person, he was revolted by the sight of his sister-in-law in dirty men's clothes, a woman grown uncontrollably wild when separated from that young person Sarah Ponsonby. What kind of crossed beast was his wife's sister? What reversal in the womb of the normal order of things could produce this . . . this monster, this weeping, violent satyr? He stared ahead as he told her Lord Butler's instructions: to convey her to Borris, and to hold her there until plans could be completed for her passage to Chambrai.

At Woodstock, Sarah was dangerously ill. The doctor found quinsy of the throat and a high fever. A vein in her foot was opened to relieve the pressure of hot, inflamed blood.

Lady Betty sent word to her daughter: 'I can't tell you how curious it all is. No man was concerned with either of them. Their plan was, I believe, no more than a scheme of romantic friendship, no more than what was fanciful and eccentric. Miss Eleanor writes three times each day to our

53

Sarah. I cannot in conscience relay such crazed sentiments to her in her state. Sarah asks constantly for word from Miss Eleanor. I tell her only she has written once to inquire of her health and sent to me her thanks. Sarah is in a state of anxiety. Twice she has fainted when I felt obliged to say that no other words than these were contained in Miss Butler's letters. My dear, write her a letter of comfort and stop the ill-natured tongues of the world.'

To herself, Sarah talks constantly: 'Why does she write nothing of her plans for us? I fear she has given me up. She thinks I am too frail for her strenuous life, too little and shallow for her large thoughts. Surely she will give me up. I will die. I am dying. I lie, like the Duke of Ormonde in Kilkenny Church, straight in my bed, an effigy in marble, my black feet on the sleek black back of an otter. Like Eleanor's ancestor, I will die of the bite to my neck by the oily beast, stretched to eternity atop my tomb, my nose cracked away, my fingers broken off at the joint by grave despoilers. No, not the bite of an otter, but instead the blast of a cannonball that removes my foolish head from my burning body. I will lie with my grandfather under the anonymous furze of the Slievnanon Hill we climbed yesterday on the way to Waterford. Or was it the day before? No, not of otter nor of cannonball. I will die of her silence.'

Lady Betty wrote to Mrs. Harriet Cavanaugh at Borris: 'I w^d be glad if you c^d prevent Miss Butler from writing so much to our Sarah. The volumes we receive here distress us. We hear Miss Butler is to be sent to a convent in France. I cann^t help but wish she had been safe in one long ago. She w^d have made us all happy.'

Margaret Cavanaugh responded to Lady Betty at once: 'It is difficult to condone my sister's actions. We plan for her to go to live in the convent as you have heard. Her family and friends are very angry with her. She will, I fear, feel forever the bad consequences of this rash and unaccountable action.'

Lady Betty felt constrained to reassure Julia Tighe, who sent again and again *to know:* 'Sarah, whose conduct has the appearance of imprudence is, I am sure, void of serious impropriety. There are no Gentlemen concerned. I can hardly think that the cause is known to anyone but themselves.'

In the afternoon she wrote again: 'No better. She talks wildly under the fever and cann' eat. In her wildness she tells me Miss Butler flew away from a convent and it is her intention to save her from Popery. She says if we knew Miss Butler we would love her as much as she does. All together it is a most extraordinary affair.'

Eleanor appeared to accept her imprisonment at Borris. She sent letters daily to Sarah. To the convent plans she listened gravely and made no response: she knew she would never go. Eleanor placed a high value upon her own ingenuity and was certain she could outwit her parents and her sluggish, provincial sister and brother-in-law. Money for passage to Chambrai and the dowry to be bestowed on Holy Sepulchre Convent upon Eleanor's arrival had arrived at Borris. Eleanor discovered it had been hidden among her sister's camisoles and planned to relieve her family of the sum when the time came. Suspecting that her letters did not arrive at her beloved's bedside, she arranged for a basket of apples and cherries from the Borris orchard to be delivered to Sarah, at the bottom of which lay a wisp of paper:

'M^y dear, I will be there today a week. Be well, and fix a place near you for me to hide. Make only small preparations so you will not be watched too closely. For escape we shall and this time we shall succeed.'

Eleanor left Borris on foot. She carried a small carpet bag, well furnished with her convent dowry and some light changes of linen. She wore handsome breeches, a warm shirt, and a cape, all removed secretly from her brother-in-law's clothes press. Her heavy boots were her own, saved from her first flight. She added a man's cap, borrowed from a servant. She felt fine, comfortable and safe as she walked the twelve miles through hill country to the river town of Inistiogue. There she stopped for food, wine, and lodging. To her delight, she was greeted as 'Sir' by the innkeeper.

Early next morning she went on to Woodstock, along the roads made dangerous by the skulking presence of the Whiteboys and the notorious Freyney. She reassured herself by thinking that the Whiteboys' targets were usually priests and tithe collectors. So determined was her gait, so confident her masculine appearance that she was not stopped. When she came to the hanging beechwood inside the entrance to Woodstock she sighed with relief: the pounds she carried in her bag would have enriched Freyney and the Whiteboys for some time.

In the dusk of early evening, Eleanor entered the house unobserved through a hall window left open for her by Sarah's maid. She found Sarah much recovered. They embraced, lingering in each other's arms, relishing the absence of the chill of separation. To their besotted eyes there was no sight in the world more welcome than the presence of the other.

*   *   *

Eleanor is weary from her two days' march. She falls
asleep almost at once. Sarah lies beside her, watching her
face, listening to her soft breathing. She finds herself
breathing in unison with her, as though they were walking
in stride. Then she dares to touch Eleanor's arm, her damp
curls, her beloved face. So it happens that frightened and
long-deprived persons, in one free moment, discover the
privileges of the body and the rewards of inconceivable
love. In one tender motion towards the other, they rejoice
in their discovery.

For two days Eleanor remained in Sarah's bedroom, eating
bread and cheese and cake smuggled to her when Sarah
returned from meals, escaping into the clothes closet at the
first sound of someone approaching in the hall. Their days
and nights were spent enjoying the luxury of their union.

But the house was not large enough and the inhabitants
too many to make concealment possible for very long. Sir
William suspected something was amiss. Perhaps it was
the absence of Sarah from her usual haunts on the stone
benches at the far recesses of the garden that made him
wonder. His suspicion that she was avoiding him brought
him one late morning unannounced to her door. There was
no time for Eleanor to enter the cupboard. They were
discovered together, reading a volume of letters by Madame de Sévigné to her daughter.

Puzzled by what to do about Lady Eleanor's presence in
her house, Lady Betty responded in the only way she
knew, by inviting her to dinner. Eleanor accepted, hungry
for a hot dinner, but sat at the table in stony silence, her

eyes averted from the despised Sir William. He recognized her coldness by going to his study immediately after supper and writing to Lord Butler. He asked him to come and remove his daughter.

Five terrible days of uncertainty and fears passed at Woodstock. Then a messenger, the solicitor Edward Parke of Kilkenny (nephew to Sarah's school mistress), brought word from Eleanor's father: Lord Butler now acknowledged the inevitable. Eleanor could leave and go where she wished as long as she did not settle in Ireland. She could take the convent monies with her. He would send a small annuity when she was settled and could provide an address. There was one unalterable condition: she was never to seek to visit any member of the family or to communicate with them so long as she should live. Eleanor bowed her head at the absoluteness of the decree, and agreed.

Lady Betty tried one final appeal to Sarah, for her conscience would not allow her to go off unwarned. While Eleanor rested one afternoon, she sought a private conference with her niece:

'Your friend has a debauched mind,' she told her. 'You will never both be able to agree if you live together. Friendship needs to be based on virtue. Yours has no such foundation and will not, I am certain, last.'

Sarah listened and made no reply.

Lady Betty wrote to her daughter: 'Anything said against Miss Butler is death to Sarah.' And when Lady Betty retired in tears to her bedroom one evening, and Eleanor said she would take her evening walk, Sir William detained Sarah and tried one last time to make a difference in her decision. Awkwardly, heavily, he fell to his knees, his Bible in one hand. With the other he grabbed Sarah's hand:

'I will never more offend you. I will double the thirty-pound allowance you now receive, if you give up this mad enterprise. Oh Sarah'—he held out his Bible—'I will never more offend you. I am sorry to have angered you, but I swear on this Holy Writ that it was not meant as you have taken it and understood it.'

'Please, Uncle, please rise.'

'It was my gallantry that you read as an annoyance.' He did not get up.

Sarah was silent. She withdrew her hand and left Sir William still on his knees. She went upstairs, where she found Eleanor, who was too concerned at Sarah's being left alone with Sir William to walk very far from the house. Eleanor took Sarah into her arms. Sarah buried her face in the rough cloth of Eleanor's riding jacket (for she had worn these clothes every day in expectation of their second flight) and cried.

'If the whole world kneeled to me as Sir William has just done, I would not alter my intention to live and die with you,' she said. Eleanor stroked Sarah's hair from her wet face and kissed her on the mouth, sealing their mutual decision in a sacrament she knew the world would surely withhold from them.

The Woodstock opposition could not withstand the sur-render of the castle or the two women's soundless but adamant resolution. More confused than convinced, the Fowneses gave in, made a promise to send £50 yearly to Sarah, and then retired to their rooms, upset and routed.

To her daughter Lady Betty sent her daily note: 'It is most extraordinary. God knows how it could be. Or how they will end.'

On the twenty-second of April, at six in the morning, eighteen days after their first attempt to achieve their freedom, they leave again, but this time without hampering by difficult plans, darkness, and illness. They are accompanied by Mary-Caryll, who happily volunteers to carry their bags and Frisk as far as Waterford. It is a fine spring morning. For the last time, they pass through the hawthorn hedge and under the great trees. Overhead, hawks wind their slow, commanding way through a flock of starlings. Sarah looks back at the gardens she has loved, at peacocks making an early morning progress from their thicket, and then, she turns quickly ahead.

Exhausted by the emotional turmoil of the past fortnight, Sir William stands at his upstairs window, watching them through half-opened eyes. They are laughing, they move rapidly along the road that curves past Woodstock toward Inistiogue. The sight of Eleanor's dark male clothes and cap, the smiling Sarah, the laden-down bulk of the maid, offend his sight. He closes his eyes on the little procession and turns away. Lady Betty is seated at the other end of the room. She refuses to witness the departure and weeps quietly into her handkerchief.

'Stop such silliness. We are well rid of her.'

Lady Betty stares at him. 'You . . . You . . .' and then cannot bring herself to finish what she had in mind to say to him.

'When that ungrateful Bruiser of a maid returns, dismiss her.'

Lady Betty replies: 'Oh yes. Of course, I had intended to do that.'

'We are well rid of them all,' he repeats and sits down heavily in his upholstered chair. His legs are painful, his head aches. He puts his foot on the high stool. 'I feel my age today, Betty,' he says.

'It is time,' she says, looking him directly in the eye.

At Waterford they bid Mary-Caryll goodbye and promise to send for her when they are settled. She tells them: 'I will then come fast, my Ladies.' They pay the fifteen guineas for each passage, murmuring at the outlay from their capital, and sail across St. George's Channel, safely avoiding the rude approaches of the American privateer, Paul Jones, landing at Milford Haven. They have decided they will travel north first, through Wales. They are sustained by the astonishing glory of each other's loving company; their hearts are set on a journey that will bring them to the haven where they plan to spend the rest of their days savouring their curious union. Their destination, they believe, is London.

Thirty days later, Sir William Fownes is stricken and starts to die. His doctors decide on bleeding until he is too weak to leave his bed. Leeches are placed on his chest, his arms and thighs and back, but the suppurating blisters raised by the cantharides cause him extreme pain. They cure nothing. He endures a week of such violence against his weakness. One night he wakes with the sense that half of him has died: speechless, blind, and paralyzed, his body is finally rid of its lubricious energies. By morning he is unconscious; he lies mercifully unaware of mortal deprivation. He does not hear Lady Betty praying at his bedside; he does not know of Death's unwelcome arrival. Death, a libertine figure not unlike Sir William himself, claims the Squire and then, as though a high price had not already been paid for all the unnatural acts of the spring, he returns to Woodstock three weeks later to take weakened and bewildered Lady Betty. Woodstock is now without squire and lady, Mary-Caryll has gone to Ross to await the Ladies' summons, and Sarah Ponsonby: where is she? Travelling the highways and towns of Wales with her beloved friend, gone from Woodstock forever.

WALES

1778–1780

Later, when they were settled, the Ladies would refer to it pleasantly as their *wanderjahr*, forgetting to add how terrible it was. Like harassed gypsies they moved from place to place, pursued by fear of poverty, even destitution, hounded by their own troubled indecision and misgivings. Where should they settle? How could they afford the high cost of life in provincial English towns? In London? They travelled in slow stages, explored with distaste the outcroppings of coal at Carmarthen in south Wales, and then went north towards Birmingham. Each village and township was considered a possible stopping place. Each was marked in Eleanor's travel book with a plus or minus sign, and then noted was the number of miles distant from London.

Later they were to think it curious that they felt no desire to consider for their settlement the alien world of Wales. In their first contact, the people seemed to them uncouth, small, too dark. The coarse bracken and heavy heather on the hills looked inhospitable, the precipitous mountains uncultivated, rude. A friendly coach driver (was not everyone they met *too* friendly, they wondered, especially the members of the serving class?) proudly pointed out to them great mounds that appeared to crop out of the Pembrokeshire hills, cromlechs of great antiquity and inexplicable heathen significance. Many believed they were stone monuments to the ancient Welsh dead. He told them legends surrounding those still-haunted megaliths, some of whose blue stones arranged in circles, he said, had been *carried* by Welshmen to Stonehenge. For five days they walked and drove about the area, listening gravely to alarming druidic myths. Merlin, the natives claimed, had made these stones dance and so ever after they were able to dance alone. The Ladies shuddered at the thought of a landscape so unreliable, so given to movement and impermanence, but they walked dutifully over the wet, windy hills and fields.

They believed very little of what they heard. But they felt it urgent that they continue to move towards England, a fertile and pleasant place, they expected, where the tongue spoken was civilised and the weather less capricious and wild. These gregarious and brutish Welsh, leading superstitious lives on their unruly landscape, made them uneasy. Mountains infested by bog and mists, lowlands rutted by dark, wooded dingles, wild streams, rivers pouring down precipitous slopes like cataracts, depthless brooks: what could two gently reared Irish Ladies find among such violences to appeal to their cultivated sensibilities? In all that rugged wasteland and great-bouldered fierce countryside (for there seemed to be almost no cities), was there a haven for them?

Finally they reached Birmingham and found a congenial

inn. At once, Sarah sent word to Sir William and Lady Betty of their address, reminding them of the allowance due, for their funds had fallen low during their month of wandering. Eleanor made no effort to inform her relatives, remembering the demeaning terms of her promise.

Comfortably lodged, but without presentable clothing, Eleanor decided they must find a tailor. Sarah wondered about the expenditure, but her companion told her they could no longer appear in public in their travel-worn and inappropriate clothing. A month had passed since their 'elopement' (as Mrs Tighe had named it to her Kilbride friends), or their 'retirement' as the Ladies themselves called the event from which they dated the beginning of their new lives. Eleanor still wore her borrowed men's outergarments and Sarah a gown she had donned on ship-board and for which she did not possess a change.

They found a fine tailor, D. D. Sutton & Son Ltd., whose windows opened on High Street. It looked to be elegant, tasteful, and, no doubt, costly. Eleanor strode into the establishment first, Sarah a step behind. The proprietor, who introduced himself as Mr Sutton the son, was well used to providing ladies with riding habits, worn by English gentry for travel by coach or horse. He greeted the two Ladies, heard their desires, and sent his sewing mistress into the disrobing room with them to take their measurements. While they were thus occupied, he set out on his broad display table the materials they might choose among. The sewing mistress fitted the Ladies for the full, plain long skirts and tight spencer jackets for which the Sutton tailors were noted. Then she suggested they step out to select their cloths.

This enterprise was to be Eleanor's, they had decided before entering the shop. Sarah agreed to wear whatever

Eleanor chose for her, for it was clear from the first that Eleanor wished them both to have the same materials.

Eleanor said: 'We shall require habits and all the accoutrements. Do you provide shirts and stocks, such things?'

'For ladies? No, my lady, but there is a fine ladies' place a square distant from here that—'

'No matter. We prefer those made for men, in suitable sizes, of course,' said Eleanor firmly.

'For ladies, yes. Of course,' said Mr Sutton the son, sounding dubious.

He gestured the Ladies back into the disrobing room. They donned plain and ruffled shirts and tried stocks and ascot neck scarfs of a variety and size suitable ordinarily to male anatomy. The sewing mistress, mystified but agreeable, made the necessary adjustments. When they returned, Mr Sutton wished to know their preference in cloth for the habits. They looked carefully over his thick bolts of black, blue, deep green, and russet worsteds, rough woollens, and fine velvets, fingering each one carefully.

Then Eleanor told Mr Sutton: 'We will have three for each of us, four in this dark blue material, two in black velvet.'

'*Six*, do you mean, my lady?'

'Six, yes. And we require cloaks, in black, of this smooth Irish tweed cloth.'

'Yes. Yes, *indeed*. It will take some time, but . . .'

'We are in no hurry except for the first sets of clothes, which we shall require when we travel soon from Birmingham. Those you may send to us at The Lark on Brewster street. We shall pay for all the work in advance. I trust you will send the remainder to us when we notify you of our permanent address.'

'Very good,' said Mr Sutton. His bland English face

betrayed nothing of his delighted astonishment at the size of the order. Never before in his memory (and he intended to ask his father, now in retirement, if *his* memory contained any such a thing) had a lady ordered more than one set of travelling clothes at a time. These ladies were . . . well, indeed, they were . . . odd.

'Riding gloves with gauntlets. Do you have those?'

'Oh yes, indeed we do.'

They each chose two pairs of fine leather gloves and then inspected Indian muslin cravats. Mr Sutton saw how things were progressing. This time he was better prepared to maintain a countenance that betrayed no surprise when Eleanor chose six for each of them. He offered them silver-tipped crops of excellent leather. They ordered two, smiling to each other at the useless but handsome acquisitions. They realized that to refuse the crops would reveal their true intentions. So they said nothing.

They were being ushered across the sill of the shop when Eleanor remembered something more.

'Hats,' she said to Mr Sutton the son.

'*Hats*, my lady? Of what variety?'

'Top hats, of beaver or silk. Perhaps both.'

A further half hour was spent discovering the Ladies' sizes and fitting to their slender heads the hats made of curved brims and high round shining tops. Four such items of headwear were ordered, two in smooth brushed beaver, two in black silk. Once again they turned to the door.

Two weeks were agreed upon as a reasonable time for the first delivery. Eleanor gave the tailor her name, preceded naturally by the title she was not entitled to, and Sarah's, the Honorable Sarah Ponsonby. She paid from the Purse that held their combined resources and they left Mr

Sutton's place, arm in arm, elated at their purchases, even though Sarah's hands shook at the thought of their extravagance. For the moment Eleanor could not concern herself with the state of their finances, so pleased was she that they had found a comfortable and satisfying costume that they could wear on all occasions, suitable, and acceptable, she was sure, to the world at large. That they meant to expand this dress to morning, afternoon, and evening use while never mounting horse or entering carriage again (for Sarah was sick of travel and fully intended when they settled to stay still in that place forever) was not revealed to the tailor.

They walked toward their inn. 'Is it possible there will be word from Woodstock about my allowance?' Sarah asked. Such an addition to their funds would go far toward mitigating the huge expenditure they had just so blithely made. Eleanor had never given the presence or absence of money a thought; she considered Sarah's concern unworthy.

A letter for Sarah waited at the innkeeper's table, from Mrs Tighe:

'Y^r letter of July the twelfth arrived the day after my mother's sad demise. I regret to inform you further that my father departed this life three weeks before my beloved mother. There can be no immediate thought of monies to you until the estate, devolving upon me and my children, is determined. Woodstock will be sold. I am sorry to send you this news, but of course you have chosen y^r path and must now walk upon it. Obediently y^{rs}. Julia Tighe.'

They departed from Birmingham in their new clothes. Again they were in search of lodgings. They thought they might try a town on the English border, Shrewsbury in

Shropshire, where, they had been told, society was warm towards Irish aristocracy. Soon after they arrived, Sarah thought to call upon Molly Hinton, who lived on High Street. She was an Irish acquaintance from Miss Parke's, where she had been, as Sarah recalled, an excellent penman. Sarah was told at the door that her old acquaintance was not at home. She left a card. They waited but received no word in return. The Ladies decided to make a last try. This time they were met at the door by the mother of Molly, who invited them in to tea and said her daughter had gone abroad to make the Tour with her great aunt Hinton. Then, somewhat abruptly, she asked if there was something she could do for Miss Sarah. The presence of Lady Eleanor and Sarah Ponsonby resplendent in royal blue velvet riding clothes and black silk beaver hats, and both clearly on foot, so stunned the mother of Sarah's schoolmate that she was not able to summon her customary amiable manners. Sarah carried with her the small greyhound, who would not be quieted without a generous helping of tea cakes.

'I am so sorry,' said Sarah. 'He is usually very well behaved.'

Mrs Hinton made no reply. Her eyes strayed to the tall hats that the Ladies had removed and placed beside them on nearby chairs. The room in which they sat was very cold, there was no fire since no guests had been expected, yet it was October. How can it have grown so late in the year, so close to winter, Eleanor wondered, sipping her tea, feeling frantic now at not being settled anywhere. Sarah occupied herself by holding Frisk's muzzle to keep him from the cake.

'How are your parents?' Mrs Hinton knew nothing about Sarah's life but assumed a young woman of her age and social status must surely be endowed with at least one parent.

'They are both dead,' said Sarah politely.

'Oh, I see. I *am* sorry. Under whose care do you live?'

'In recent years with Sir William and Lady Betty Fownes of Woodstock. Sadly they are this spring deceased.'

'That *is* sad. Will you remain in England or return to our dear country?' Mrs Hinton's conversation was pointedly directed to Sarah, nonplussed as she was by the unexplained presence of the lordly Lady Eleanor.

'We are not sure. We are deciding upon a place to settle, a home, before the winter quite sets in.' Sarah's eyes sought Eleanor's, asking her silently to intervene somehow in these explanations. Bored with Mrs Hinton, Eleanor sat in what seemed to Sarah to be disapproving silence.

'Shrewsbury,' (she pronounced it 'Shrosebury') said Mrs Hinton, 'can be very pleasant in the spring. It is of course not Dublin. There is nothing like Dublin in the spring, but we are on the road to it, so we see our friends on their way to London.'

'How many miles is "Shrosebury" to London?' asked Eleanor.

'I'm not quite sure. Two days' journey by coach I know.'

'Do you go often to London?' asked Eleanor. 'Is Molly well?' asked Sarah. The Ladies spoke at once, one on top of the other.

'Very well. She is to be married in the spring to Mr Colwin Grant-Morris, who is an English barrister but very nice, very thoughtful, very well established in his profession. Her great aunt wished to give her the Tour of Europe before she settled down in London.' Mrs Hinton's complaisance at being able to communicate this news was clear to the Ladies.

'How very nice.' Sarah's small store of conversation was close to depletion. Eleanor recognized the symptoms and decided, valiantly, to try again.

'Do you go often to London?' she asked.

'Seldom. The roads, as you must have discovered, are atrocious. Everywhere we are in danger of footpads. The stagecoach is slow but safer, so we rarely use our carriage.'

Eleanor's patience was at an end. She had had enough of Mrs Hinton. She stood up, placed her cup resolutely on the tea-table, offered her hand to Sarah, who took it and also rose. Together they presented a perplexing tableau to Mrs Hinton. 'Thank you,' Eleanor said to Mrs Hinton, who watched, fascinated, as the two Ladies restored their silk hats to their cropped, powdered heads. She led them to the door, mumbling something about telling Molly of their visit when she returned from Switzerland. Sarah thanked her.

'A terrible, terrible bore,' said Eleanor. 'We shall not make such visits again.'

'No. I regret I thought of Molly Hinton. At school she seemed somehow . . .'

'And what is more, we shall not settle in . . . in Shrosebury.'

Sarah laughed and pressed Eleanor's arm in agreement. They walked back along High Street, their footsteps in unison, as always.

*   *   *

Once more they went on the road, travelling in a northerly direction towards Ellesmere. To save wear on their new clothes, and because it was not conceivable to them to save money by riding outside, they paid the extra two shillings two pence and obtained inside seats.

English stages were commodious. Ten persons shared their interior, rather more on top, and six horses moved the vehicle. The Ladies were assessed for every thirty miles of their trip because their luggage was so heavy. To this cost Eleanor raised aristocratic objections, but the drivers were adamant and collected the tax.

At Ellesmere they stayed at the inn where the coach stopped to change horses. Sarah was weary. Eleanor decided they should rest in their room for two days, asking for their meals there. Sarah slept badly because, she said, she was disturbed by her dreams. For some time, Eleanor had noticed an odd fact: Sarah's dreams often extended into waking hours. Now, seated at the table before the window, looking out over the green wooded hills that ringed Ellesmere and the large mere to the east of their windows, Sarah's face was wet with tears. Eleanor watched her covertly, seated beside her and composing a letter to Lady Adelaide, who, she had now decided, must be reached concerning the depletion of their monies.

'What troubles you, my love?'

Startled, Sarah gazed at Eleanor for a moment and then assured her it was nothing, 'a dream, nothing more than that.'

So great was Eleanor's contentment with Sarah that she could not imagine herself as the source of Sarah's disturbance.

'Tell me what you are thinking. Are you unhappy with me?'

'No. Oh, *no*. Not unhappy a bit, my love.' Forced by Eleanor's doubts to explain, she confessed to her one of her persistent visions:

'It happened to me this afternoon while I rested on the bed. I awakened to discover that the ceiling had been lowered until it stretched across me, resting on my nose and my upturned toes. The sides of the room slid towards me and touched the top of my head and the soles of my feet. I discovered that this bed on which I lay had stiffened, forming a board against my back. I was coffined,' she told Eleanor as the tears poured down her face. 'I lay there, boxed in, my eyes open, my heart beating violently against the walls of my chest, my hands stiff and useless at my sides. Dead. No, not dead quite. Buried alive. Dead and alive at the same time, *buried*,' she told Eleanor. Now she was sobbing.

Eleanor stood behind Sarah's chair, reached down and enfolded her in her arms, her hands caressing her breasts. 'Oh my dear love,' she said, 'you are alive, more alive than anyone I have known in this life. Do not think of death. It was a fancy, a dream, nothing more.'

'No. I think not. I was awake. It must have happened, truly.'

'Tush. Tush. It never happened. It will not happen.'

That night they lay close together, Sarah's face against Eleanor's arm. 'I have a favor to ask,' Sarah said.

'Of course, anything, my dearest.'

'Promise you will be sure I am dead before you allow me to be put in a coffin and into the ground.'

Eleanor laughed. But Sarah closed her eyes. Her arm

thrown across Eleanor's breast stiffened in anger. 'Please, Eleanor, promise me.'

'I promise. I'll do even more to put your mind at rest. I have heard of a device invented by a man in County Cork. It was for a friend of his who, like you, was fearful of premature burial. A cord was to be tied to the man's thumb, then brought out through a boring in his coffin and attached to a bell in his wife's chamber. Its intent was to warn his wife of any movement within the coffin, should he awaken after being confined to it. Even after burial in the ground, it was to remain attached.'

'For how long?'

'For a long time, I believe. A fortnight or longer.'

'Did it . . . work?'

'Of that, my love, I have no knowledge. But I promise you the same arrangement in the unlikely event that I am here when you require it. Does that relieve your mind?'

'Yes. I thank you for it.' Sarah continued to stare ahead, her eyes fixed on Ellesmere's yellow plain. Already the trees were losing their leaves. Coarse hay stood in unruly piles awaiting the harvest.

'What is it? Is there more?'

'No. Yes. I do not understand how it could have happened today.'

'But it did not happen. You dreamed—'

'Oh yes, my love, it happened. It did.'

In Eleanor's travelbook: 'Oswestry, Wales: Sarah begins to sleep well, to my relief. She seems free of dreams. We are told of effigies in the parish church who kneel for all eternity, but we did not walk to see them. In this town flannel, called by the inhabitants *gwlan*, in their strange

tongue, is woven on winter evenings by the farmers who
have sheep. We are invited to visit a family. We look in
upon them when they are seated in their large kitchen. One
woman is engaged in spinning. Another knitting. A young
man, a cousin, we are told, carves wooden spoons for
ladles. Another works upon a token to be given to his
betrothed. This he calls a 'lovespoon,' for two spoons
hang side by side from a single ornamented panel fancily
designed with hearts and flowers. The father, resting from
his labours, reads aloud from *The Black Book of Carnar-*
then in the barbaric language spoken here. A daughter is in
the corner playing upon a three-stringed harp. I am delighted at the sound. I think I w^d like such an instrument
for myself. Sarah orders a set of lovespoons to be made for
us with our initials cut into the panel. The son promises to
stop his work and do ours tomorrow for, once more, we
are to travel on.'

Quite by accident, in Oswestry, the Ladies encountered
Miss Harriet Bowdler, a spinster who claimed to remember Lady Eleanor Butler from their mutual attendance at a
Rotunda Ball in Dublin. She rushed to intercept them
when she saw them walking across the road to their inn.

'I am *certain* you are Lady Eleanor Butler of Kilkenny,'
she cried in a high thin voice, made even more penetrating
because now, close up to the curiously clad woman, she
was not sure at all. This person looked somehow different,
she thought, a combination of staunch male bust for the top
half, full feminine pudicity from the hips down. And the
twin lady? Could this be her infamous friend?

'I am,' said Eleanor to her, coldly. 'I regret I do not
remember—'

'Miss Harriet Bowdler. And this is . . . ?'

'This is my dear friend, the Honorable Sarah Ponsonby.'

'Of course. How do you do, Miss Ponsonby.'

After they exchanged the necessary introductory details and identifications (try as she would Eleanor could not remember this person or the ball for which Miss Bowdler seemed to have such admirable recall), Harriet invited them to her house, close by, and Sarah nodded yes before Eleanor could frame a refusal.

Miss Harriet Bowdler lived alone with the overpowering and omnipresent memory of her mother. Lady Jane Bowdler had died two years before, leaving Harriet a house and a small competence, somewhat more modest than her beloved only child had anticipated (she confessed to the Ladies) but enough, she hastened to add, to permit her to live exactly as had her mother after her husband's death.

At dinner in the small house with Harriet that last evening in Oswestry, the Ladies felt they could sense Lady Jane's presence in every move of her well-dressed, solidly built daughter. Her features were pert and shapely but too close to the centre of the perfect circle of her face. Her red hair, in matronly fashion, was bound tightly in a bun of curls. She was distinguished by her possession of a considerable amplitude of bosom, hip, and backside. Her pumpkin shape was layered in material that rustled as she walked. A portrait of her mother above the mantel betrayed how strong was Harriet's maternal genetic lineage.

'I miss her,' Harriet confided to the Ladies, seeing Eleanor's eyes on the portrait. 'But, living here where she lived, I feel her presence very strongly.'

Sarah looked up at the dimpled, heavy face of Lady Jane Bowdler and studied her cap of carefully painted lace and white curls. Except for the colour of the hair, Harriet might have been speaking of herself.

'Living alone seems to age one faster,' she said, fingering the rings of flesh about her neck. 'One's days are often wearisome. I am so glad you were able to dine with me.'

The Ladies smiled politely. Sarah seemed bemused. Eleanor followed her eyes as she inspected one after the other of the Bowdler portraits that covered the walls of the dining room. Harriet rambled on, talking of Dublin, whist games, county fairs. Suddenly Sarah was in tears. Eleanor left her place at the table, took her hand, and led her to a corner of the room. Harriet Bowdler hovered about them, horrified.

'What have I said? What have I done?'

'Nothing at all. Pay no heed,' Eleanor said, trying to place herself between their massive hostess and Sarah's discomposure. 'Miss Ponsonby is very tired. We must return to our lodgings.' Harriet Bowdler, rustling noisily as she walked, led them to the door, chattering her farewells.

At the inn Sarah went to bed at once without saying anything about her spell. Eleanor did not question her. She had begun to realise that behind Sarah's charming young face there dwelled a demon that inflamed and sometimes governed her, but whose nature was unknown to her, a moving, dread spirit that drove her into caverns where Eleanor could not follow.

The next morning Eleanor asked: 'My love, are you longing for Ireland?'

Sarah shook her head. 'Not Ireland, my beloved, but Woodstock, I sometimes think. The gardens, the shrubberies, the great trees, the fields . . .'

'But what of Sir William? Do you not recall his . . . importuning?'

Sarah looked at her in confusion. 'Sir William?'

'You must still be weary, my love. Tell me, is it a place, a home you mourn for?'

'It must be so. Last night I thought, for no reason, of how separated we are from everyone, from every place we've ever known. I am glad, happy, to be always with you. But for that moment, as we sat surrounded by all the Bowdlers, I felt we were both homeless orphans. Disconnected persons.'

'We are alone *together*, are we not?'

Sarah nodded, her eyes fixed on Eleanor as though she was trying to see her as a rock she could lean upon. She did not reply.

Eleanor put down her tea cup and took Sarah's face between her hands, moving her fingers over her soft cheeks. 'Sarah, my love, we shall soon have a place, a home. I promise you. We'll live together as married persons do. We'll live and love as they do. Love has no sex, my dearest. We'll live in our own cottage when we find one. You are not orphaned; you are mine. You belong to me. I am yours. Don't you see that?'

Sarah cried. Then she said: 'Yes. Yes. I see that.'

Eleanor recognised the painful truth: their wanderings must cease at once. They would have to settle quickly in some quiet, isolated place, where they could be safe, near people who knew nothing of their history, where they could be whatever it was they were, without question or challenge.

'Oswestry: 172 miles from London,' Eleanor put down in her book.

*   *   *

They planned the thirty-mile journey the next day, from Ellesmere north and west across the River Dee and into the valley village of Llangollen, intending to 'make' Holyhead, a distance of more than one hundred and sixty miles, before Christmas. Holyhead protruded like a tortoise head from Holy Island, a spit of land directly across from Dublin. Sarah, as she admitted to Eleanor, longed for Ireland, for the ordered and settled paths of Woodstock, the familiar flowers and shrubberies around its gardens. It was she who wished to push on to Holyhead. She told Eleanor that a homesick Irish maid at the Queen's Inn in Oswestry where they lodged for some weeks had told her that if one stood on the very tip of Caergybi and peered across the South Irish Sea one might see the outskirts of Baile Atha Cliath.

'Of *where*?' Sarah had asked her.

The maid had replied, with some scorn in her voice, 'Of Dublin.'

'Do you believe it is possible, Eleanor?'

'I do not. Those are rough seas, rarely without their fog and heavy mists. And the distance must be fifty miles.'

The last night at the inn in Ellesmere they made their pact. In their ultimate account of their history, it came to be a time and place in which their lives were shaped. They spoke of it as Moses may have recalled Pisgah, a high point from which they saw their future home without knowing it was so close, so assured.

Before going to bed they packed their clothes for early departure. Then they sat in straight chairs opposite each other, their knees touching, leaning forwards so their hands could be clasped. The heavy musk of their woollen habits hung in the air between them, uniting them in a single bodily miasma. Their postures were the same. Still, the heavy seriousness of Eleanor's countenance, the sixteen years she had beyond Sarah's youth made her seem a school mistress and Sarah her sweet-faced, smiling, compliant pupil.

Except for the monetary cloud that followed them everywhere, Eleanor's happiness was complete. She possessed Sarah, in a way and to a depth she did not herself fully comprehend. During her forty years she had felt yearnings that kept her away from the well-marked pathways of marriage. But where she walked, her unique path, was a .mystery to her. Repelled by the characters and the flesh of men, she was still not open to the suggestion, as were her parents, of a sterile existence in conventual celibacy. There was settled on her chest, boring deep into the core of herself, an ache that her legs could not walk off, a burning about the bones that seemed to sear the hinges of her skeleton, as though her layers of skin and flesh were protecting a mysterious fire she could not extinguish or explain to herself. She loved. She wanted to be loved. Who? By whom? Until she saw the schoolgirl Sarah Ponsonby, she did not associate her yearning with another person, except to know where it could not rest: on her parents or sister, on the pursuant Lord Kilbriggin. Her childhood preference in clothing and hair dressing suggested nothing to her except the convenience of a boy's fortunate freedom. She had always wondered why she wished to resemble in her dress a sex she could not love.

But Sarah: in her she found the object she had desired, not knowing what it was she sought. Seeing Sarah she knew at once that here was the subject of her daydreaming. Now there was a form, a sex, to the shadowy figure. She was content, as though her life required nothing more than this positive identification.

For Sarah there was greater confusion. Her doubts shaped her nightmares and her waking fantasies. Was she a freak of nature without human precedent? Was this love into which she had entered so greedily a frightful and debauched Thing, a gorgon of desire and satiety? Were she and Eleanor curiosities? Could it be that their union was contrived by the Devil to punish those who ran from the attentions of the Sir Williams of the world? Her love for Eleanor filled her life and the early moments of her sleep before her terrors took over. Yet there were times when she felt strangely alone and set apart even from Eleanor. Was their unparalleled union a work of art or a witches' brew? The action of a vindictive hag against the errant human race? She knew no answers to her questions and no place to look for them, no one she could ask.

Sarah, like Eleanor, had been entirely innocent of love. But she possessed a loving soul, a part of herself that seemed to float free of objects in search of a place to light ever since the time of her early losses. With relief and instant recognition she had settled her love on Eleanor. Her confusion had not been allayed by this act: What did this alliance *mean*? she wondered. How did it fit into the patterns of conduct taught and demonstrated to her by Miss Parke, by Lady Betty, by Mrs Tighe? How did it look to them? To the world?

In the evening before their departure from the Ellesmere Inn, as they sit opposite each other, holding each other's hands tightly and contemplating their future, Sarah is able to suspend her doubts. It is a time of rare wordless understanding. Their hearts are full. They feel that their bodies have lost their distinguishing marks and become one. Eleanor sighs with contentment and tightens her fingers over Sarah's. A fantasy of the heart arises in their breasts, a vision entirely without sexual topography, a landscape composed of themselves floating free of bodily organs, a place without persons where what they feel for each other, like a yellow mist, like a warm fog, flows over the glowing interior of their land.

Sarah sits still, entranced. But Eleanor's pragmatic mind moves rapidly from epiphanic moments to decisions and plans.

Eleanor speaks: 'When we settle, we must write a program for our lives. What we vow we shall do and what we know we shall not do. Surely we want none of the foolish comings and goings our families indulged in. What have we to do with such settlements down into ordinary life?'

Sarah wonders: 'Shall we promise never to leave our cottage, when we have found it, except in each other's company?'

Eleanor says: 'That is necessary, yes. And further, we'll vow not to stay a night under another's roof, once we are established under our own.'

Eleanor goes on: 'We must improve ourselves.'

Sarah, surprised: 'How?'

Eleanor: 'We'll read together and talk with each other about what we have read. I shall keep a record of our reading and our opinions. We must cultivate languages so that our reading may widen: Italian, French, German. We must learn those languages together.'

Sarah says: 'I want to make where we live beautiful. To plant something beautiful in every place our eyes light upon from our windows and along the borders of our place. We shall plant gracefully and with love. I want so much to have gardens, to nurture them, then to bring the results into our house as though there were no interruption between the outside and within.'

Sarah goes on: 'What shall we do about the world outside?'

Eleanor, ponderously: 'Eschew it and all its vanities. Those effeminate softnesses are not for us.'

Sarah: 'We shall not go out into society?'

Eleanor: 'No, we shall wait for society, if it so wishes, to come to us. And then we will welcome only those of high degree, and who will contribute to our self-improvement or our entertainment. Persons like ourselves.'

A long pause.

Then Sarah asks, timidly, almost whispering: 'Are there other persons like ourselves?'

Eleanor, at once: 'I speak of breeding and education, not . . . not anything else. As for that . . . I do not know. I have never met others. Or heard of them. Perhaps. We shall see.'

Eleanor continues: 'When we are in full possession of our monies we must practice charity. In our retirement, we must perform the duties of our birth, even to foreigners, should we decide to live among them.'

Sarah: 'And kind. We must always be kind. We must send for Mary-Caryll at once, else she will forget her intentions towards us and go into service elsewhere.'

Sarah goes on: 'Painting, drawing, embroidery. I shall return to the practise of those arts which gave me such pleasure at school. And you must continue to write. Your letters to me at school were so fine. You must be our correspondent, and our diarist.'

Eleanor: 'Our retirement from the world will be rich and

full, else we will look for other diversions and perhaps grow apart.'

Sarah: 'Oh never, my love. That could never happen.'

Sarah hesitates, then continues: 'We might make room each day for reading in the Gospels and the old books of Holy Writ.'

Eleanor: 'No.'

Sarah: 'Never, do you mean, my love? What then will be our guide in spiritual matters? "There shall be no authority except God's Will," Saint Paul told the Romans.'

Eleanor: 'We shall be our own guides. Our own wills have taken us this far. Church authority is best left for those weak enough to be bound by empty sacraments from priests, like my poor mother. They are not for us. Ours is . . . a new way. We need no one's approval. We'll not ask for a sacramental seal to our love. We shall make no explanations to anyone, no confessions, ask for no absolutions.'

Sarah: 'No explanations?'

Eleanor: 'None.'

PLAS
NEWYDD

1780–1790

*L*ate the next day they came by stagecoach to the small village of Llangollen in the County Clwyd, a word they could spell but not, at first, pronounce. They took a room at The Hand, because they admired the two-storey grey stone public house and the view from their room of small houses of dark stone. Early in the morning they set out on foot to see the village and the surrounding country. Spanning the rushing River Dee were four Gothic arches of ancient stone, a warm-appearing solid bridge that suggested to them an unchanging reverberant past as they crossed, hand in hand. They climbed a conical hill until they arrived at the ruins of old Crow Castle. Beside the ruins ran a deeply wooded dingle and through it a rapid stream moved. They were along at Castell Dinas Bran, as the place was named, so they took off their heavy shoes and bathed their feet in the cold water.

Beyond the ruins was heaped a long line of limestone rocks, so tempting to the foot that Sarah climbed them, holding her riding skirt in her hand. Eleanor stood at the bottom watching, enjoying the sight of her beloved friend stepping from crest to peak in long, graceful steps.

Arm in arm, they retraced their steps and then took the way along the canal towing-path out past a flagstone quarry until they came to mouldering church ruins, lying snug in a quiet and most beautiful dale. A small sign said this was Llan Eglewest Abbey. A villager gathering mushrooms along the sheepwalks and among the graves of long-dead Cistercian monks told them it was now called Valle Crucis and had been built around 1200.

'How long have the monks been gone?' asked Eleanor.

'Since King Henry took the gold and silver things and sent the monks no one knows where. Two hundred years ago maybe.'

The villager left with his basket full of soil-colored mushrooms. The Ladies rested, leaning upon the decaying broken stones, alone together in the silent courtyard of the abbey, in the shadow of the steep hill that rose above the monastery remains. The sentimental hearts of the two women were prone to emotional responses to ancient buildings in ruins, if not to the religious aura of the place. They kissed, a long, loving kiss, and then stood apart and looked at each other.

They walked back along the abbey road, their arms upon each other, moved by having witnessed the half-destroyed Gothic aspirations of monks. Re-crossing the beautiful old bridge, they followed cobbled Bridge Street to the Church of St. Collen, and stood back to admire its carved roof. The sacristan came out to tell them that it had been carried from the abbey and held aloft by Welshmen of great spiritual and physical gifts until it was placed upon the walls of the parish church.

Late in the day, as they walked south of the village on Hill Street, to visit Pengwern Hall, a deserted old mansion they had been told was picturesque, they came upon the cottage. No one seemed to occupy it. It stood in a vale from one side of which rose the blue Berwyn mountain dotted with sheep. A plain two-storey, square structure, its tile roof held five chimneys. The surface stone was white-washed. The Ladies tried to look into the windows, but in the dying light they could see very little except that the rooms seemed empty of furnishings. One of the windows was broken. They thought, standing close, that they could hear the flap of bat wings.

'Can this be the place?' Sarah asked. 'Would we like it here?'

'In this house? In this vale? I believe so. Let's inquire of the people in the village who own it and if it is available to rent.'

Mrs Edmunds of The Hand was a well of information. Recently widowed, she was lonely and loved to talk. Her monologues were filled with complaints as well as vivid descriptions of Llangollen sights. First, she bemoaned the absence of her husband and the difficulty of raising children and keeping an inn without a man to do the heavy work. Then she urged upon them a walk out Canal Road to the Tower. They ate their chops and goose tarts in silence, waiting patiently for the answer to their question about the cottage. 'The Tower is twelve feet high and named Eliseg's Pillar,' Mrs Edmunds told them. 'He was slain by Saxons in the seventh century and his father then erected it in his memory. I believe. It stands on a tumulus which may be his grave. We believe so.'

The Ladies were afraid to ask why the Saxons had committed the act, fearing the question would take the garrulous Mrs Edmunds too far from their original query. Finally, she came back to their subject. She recognised that her boarders were ladies of high degree, oddly clothed, it was true, but of a station well above the people of the village, or even of nearby Ruthin and Berwyn. True, it was strange that they were both without husbands: Were they spinster sisters, or congenial cousins? she wondered. But they clearly intended to be domiciled together, nonetheless, or they would not have inquired about the cottage. She acknowledged to herself that surely none of this concerned her. She gave them the name and location of the owner, and said she hoped they would stay on at The Hand until they found lodgings to rent, and not venture into the cold and unclean Lyons Inn across the road.

So they did. The summer months were spent awaiting or overseeing repairs and changes to the cottage. With Mr Edwards, the owner, a gruff and incommunicative old Welsh farmer who had retired to his daughter's cottage in Chirk, they settled upon a yearly rent of £22, and were granted permission to make extensive changes they themselves would pay for. At once a painter, a carpenter, and a joiner were hired. Eleanor drew plans for the improvements. A room, to serve as library, was to be added to the four already there. Water was to be brought into the kitchen from the hillside stream. Their dressing room upstairs was to be formed of the old nursery. The 'state' bedchamber for their guests was to be widened, and a small maid's room constructed where open sheds now stood behind the kitchen. Chests and cabinets were ordered from the joiner, who would make them for the carpenter to

decorate in their places. Mary-Caryll was on her way to
Plas Newydd.

The Ladies were worn down from incessant travel, the
emotional strain of their escapes, and by the constant
worry over monies. Two years after their elopement, they
and their maid Mary-Caryll, with all the heavy, ornamented carved oak furniture they had ordered in Oswestry,
were moved into the cottage they named Plas Newydd, the
New Place. It was the fall of 1780. Despite their weariness, their sense of their strange, unique mission buoyed
them. Their apostolic zeal for a way of life they believed
they had devised for the first time in the history of the
world was very strong. As William Wordsworth, forty
years later, was to write of them: They were about to
'retire into notice.'

It was the first home the Ladies had ever had. For
Eleanor, Kilkenny Castle was where she had waited impatiently to be grown enough to leave, even when she
could not imagine how such a departure could be effected
without ending in the novitiate or in marriage. At Woodstock Sarah had believed she held her room on Sir William's impatient sufferance. She was an orphan, at the
mercy of those who lent her space, her room, her hiding
places in the garden. But Plas Newydd was the place they
had chosen to remake into their ideal of home. A cave of
oak and stone, it was designed to safeguard the privity of
their love.

During the first year of their residence no one visited
Plas Newydd. This suited their desires exactly; they had
promised to be alone with each other. Word of their flight
and their occupancy at Llangollen had spread in English
circles to which both families were connected, and to
Ireland when Eleanor sent a beseeching letter for money to

her mother and because Sarah maintained a lively correspondence with her cousin Julia Tighe. Travellers to Dublin and back to London who passed through Llangollen
knew that the Ponsonby woman and the curious Lady of
Ormonde lineage were there but did not venture to call,
some of them out of reluctance to enter upon the embar-
rassing mystery of their lives.

It happened, by pure chance, that the Ladies had settled
in a place likely to bring visitors to their door. The highway from London went north and west to Oxford and
thence to Birmingham and on to Shrewsbury and Llangollen.
The stage coach made a stately swath through Llangollen's
small main street, depositing visitors to the outlying man-
ors at The Hand or The Lion's Inn, and then went on to
Holyhead, where a steamer carried the English travellers to
Dublin. It returned with Irish gentry (in the main) on their
way to stays among the social pleasures of London.

Quickly, the routine the Ladies had agreed upon was
established. They never deviated: it was as though a single
exception would shake the whole structure of their exceptional lives. They lived strictly and carefully, rarely leaving the Place.—Mary-Caryll went to the market in the
village less than a mile away, visiting the grocery lady,
Mrs Parry the greengrocer, the baker, and the butcher.
Sometimes she took the borrowed cob as far as Bryn
Kivalt to the lady who sold cheese; astride the small horse
she looked huge and brought smiles to the faces of villagers. The market men soon learned to fear her tart tongue
and ready, rough hand. She was as large and as strong as
any man in the village. She wished to be called Miss
Mary, she informed them, and the tradesmen and farmers
(from whom she obtained eggs, milk, cream, and buttermilk) were quick to obey. The man who brought beers and

ales to The Hand remembered her well from her Irish employment.

'They used to call her Mary the Bruiser,' he told Mrs Edmunds. 'Many's the time I saw her haul out customers from Inistiogue pub at closing time when they got out of hand, sometimes two at a time.' The Ladies could not have had a better guardian of their retirement, a protector against beggars and unwanted visitors. A woman of noticeable and intimidating masculinity, Mary-Caryll provided muscular protection of her Ladies against intruders, the insobriety of the town's boys, and the temptation of the tradesmen to scale their prices upwards for gentry.

One day in November, after almost half a year in seclusion, they decided upon an extended walk beyond their hedge and away from the customary circuit of the New Place they took each morning and evening. Asking at the inn, where Mrs Edmunds was delighted to see them again, they were directed by the lady, who tried to detain them with her cascading river of talk, to Mr Turner the barber, whose cottage stood on a small road beside the river. The Dee was high and wild at that time of year. It tore through the middle arch of the bridge rasping against the fourteenth-century stones and creating an excited melody of turbulent sounds.

'It must be very deep where it passes under the bridge,' Sarah said. She stooped to look over, and then gripped the side. 'Often I dream of being bourne along on such a violent stream.

'Mrs Edmunds, who seems to know everything about this village, said in this season it is twenty feet,' said Eleanor, pushing at Sarah's elbow to move her along. She had noticed her friend's tendency to dwell overlong at high cliffs, bridges, and threatening streams as though the prospect of falling from them was enticing. Sarah stared a long time into the rushing river. 'At Woodstock the stream only covered one's ankles. Here, one might be . . . submerged.' Eleanor did not reply. It had been a long time since Sarah had had a spell. She thought they were over, that the New Place with its calm security had worked a cure.

'Come along, my love, we must be on our way.'

They found the cottage of Mr Turner and instructed him in the manner in which they wished to have their hair barbered and dressed. Eleanor's hair was now grey, Sarah's still bright brown. The barber was told to cut their hair short, so that it fell no lower than their ears, in what Eleanor called the 'Titus-style.' Mr Turner followed their orders precisely. When he had finished, their heads resembled two deep porridge bowls, he thought. He curled the ends and powdered their short Irish curls (as he thought of them). They left his cottage, well pleased with the results, having arranged for him to come to their cottage to dress their hair every fortnight. Their high silk hats set on their heads, they provided the villagers with what they were to call, at the Pub that evening, 'a sight.' They might have been twin coachmen or perhaps two elderly priests making their way to call upon ailing parishioners.

As for Mr Turner, he felt he had made a major advance in his profession. For the first time in forty-seven years at his trade he had barbered the heads of women. He smiled as he swept the mat of hair on his floor. How strange this day's business was: to cut *two* women's hair on the same afternoon and to cut it to make them look exactly like gentlemen! . . . Who, he wondered, was Titus?

*   *   *

In the first year at Plas Newydd the Ladies added six
Welsh mountain sheep to their demesne, a word Eleanor
used ironically for their four acres of rented property. The
sheep were hardy, active animals for whom Sarah conceived a great affection. She named them carefully according to what she conceived to be their characters, and
enjoyed caressing their soft wool and cradling the ewes in
her arms. They were tame and loving, their joints supple,
their bones as small as young children's. Sarah bought a
brindled, white-breasted greyhound to accompany them on
their walks with Frisk, who had grown old and no longer
earned his name. The new hound, almost white and as thin
as a walking stick, she named Flirt and trained to sleep on
the end of their bed: poor Frisk could no longer make the
leap. From the carpenter's wife they came by a kitten of
such varied colours and ancestry that Sarah named him
Tatters. And for Mary-Caryll's use they purchased a cob, a
short-legged, stocky and, at first, overactive little horse.
He was tethered on the hill among the sheep and quickly
acquired some of their ruminative complaisance. Even so,
Eleanor shuddered at the sight of him: Never again would
she mount a horse, even a steady little Welsh cob.

Except for Mary-Caryll, Love, Charity, Pride, Faith,
Hope, Patience (the sheep), Nathan, the cob, and the two
greyhounds, the Ladies were alone. With scrupulous care
they boxed and contained their units of time, enjoying
such highly organised solitude. They began by learning
three useful Welsh words each day from a primer they had
ordered from Wrexham ('O, the luxury of buying books,'
Eleanor wrote in her day book upon the arrival of the
package). They found that Wales was properly called *Cymru*,

the people of *Cymru* the *Cymry,* the word for mourning at a loss, *hiraeth.* From another new volume, they studied the Bronze-Age history of the stone circles, menhirs, and cromlechs they had seen in Pembrokeshire. For the Tuatha De Danaan, the Celtic myths on which they had been nurtured, they began to substitute those of the Tylwyth Teg and the history of the *Cymry* who lived west of the eighth-century King Offa's Dike. The *Cymry* were the people among whom they had chosen to live.

After Mrs Tighe's eighty-pound sum had arrived for the year, their first large expenditure was for a New Bed. Their second-storey bedroom was large and held a fine bay window plated with decorative glass and lined with carved oak at the sides. The Bed was built into one side so that an oak-panelled wall became its headboard. The early morning sun reached their pillows as they slept. At the foot were two rich oak posts holding aloft the corners of the rectangular tester. From it hung a heavy moreen curtain. They lay upon a well-packed and covered palliasse and were blanketed in soft-woven woollens they had had sent from Ireland. The New Bed was a protected, stable, private ark, nestled snugly against a wall that had been covered with blossom-embossed paper.

The day, which usually ended in what Eleanor called, in her day book, 'sweet peace in the New Bed,' began in strict order. They rose at six with the first sun (there were to be exceptions) and walked together in their garden. At nine they breakfasted, sometimes at the kitchen table, at other times, when they wished to prolong their united solitude, at the table in the State Bedroom. Mary-Caryll prepared their food and served it but always, when they invited her, politely refused to sit with them to eat her breakfast, claiming she had already partaken. For them she poured tea into a saucer and served them *Posel Triog*, a treacle posset of boiled fresh milk to which she added cold buttermilk. It was a Welsh dish she had learned about from her friend, the cook at The Hand. Sarah loved it and called it curds and whey.

'Which is exactly what it is, of course,' Eleanor would say.

'Di olch yn faur,' said Sarah, proud of her Welsh for 'Thank you very much.'

Or Mary-Caryll would serve them what the Welsh countrywomen called *Siencyn Tea*, pouring hot tea over white-flour bread and adding butter and sugar and then a little fresh, cold milk. They would eat this with slices of thick white cheese, drink their tea, and then set out for a brisk walk to some part of the village, or make a much slower tour of their own grounds. While Eleanor dictated, Sarah took notes in her elegant hand on what they saw needed doing: Mr Hughes the gardener came (at first) only one day in the week to do heavy work. They would sit in the shrubberies to decide what might be substituted for the common overgrown yews and filberts they had found there. Their planning conferences were held as they walked 'the Home Circuit': Where would the new fowl yard be put? The new dairy? Should the gravel paths be extended? What soft-fruit trees ought to be planted and where, so that they might, in the future, have a ready supply of wines?

The adjective for their possessions the Ladies most relished was 'new.' For them the word had a strong attraction because they thought of their union as new, unique, without precedent. At times Eleanor would refer to it as a 'New marriage.' They had named their cottage Plas Newydd; familiarly with each other they spoke always of 'our New Place.'

Lady Adelaide made no response to Eleanor's increasingly importuning letters. Nonetheless, the two friends agreed on large, lavish expenditures and then gave them no further thought: they were granted unlimited credit, it seemed to them, by workmen and tradesmen who were in awe of Eleanor's title. At all costs, the Ladies were determined to enrich the quality of their lives. But, in a small concession to weight and economy, their lunch at twelve was spartan: cheese, an egg, fruit, tea. Often they carried it in a basket and ate under a tree or on one of the benches the carpenter had made for them. After other excursions, beyond their 'demesne,' to the Tower, or the church, or Valle Crucis, or Dinas Bran, they returned home to rest.

They became ardent, indurate walkers, always wearing their heavy ploughman's boots, always carrying their silver-topped walking sticks, always accompanied by their dogs, always alone together. Although Eleanor deplored the rapidity with which they wore down their boots and the cost of having them repaired by the village cobbler, Sarah continued to climb the hills, the Trevor rocks, and the precipices on the Eglwyseg mountains. Her attraction to heights accompanied her fear that she might be tempted to leap. Each time, she went grimly aloft to experience the possibility of a fall.

Often, on the road back to Plas Newydd, they would wave to their neighbours, Matthew the miller, the weaver Robert, the coal dealer John Williams, but never, in that first year, did they stop to speak. To the villagers, who gossiped a great deal about them over their beers at the Hand, they were the Vale Ladies who did not, oddly, indulge themselves like other gentry at gaming tables, at country balls, and race-meetings. They seemed indifferent to summer visits to Llangammarch or Llanwrtyd Wells, the popular watering places. Wherever they walked they were observed: on the hills like two stout black sheep, on the streets, at the ruins and the rocks. To their neighbours, they seemed to be one person endowed with more than the usual number of appendages and heads, peculiarly garbed in their habits and high hats, conspicuously together.

In season they stopped to watch young children picking stray white wool out of the brambles. At first, they attended the dipping and shearing of their own beloved sheep. The farmer David Morris drove their animals to his dipping vats. They would follow behind to witness the annual process, empathising with Patience and Hope and the others as they were held, painfully Sarah was sure, under their tender front legs and lowered into the vats.

'Oh poor Charity,' Sarah cried in her anguish.

'It bothers them not a bit, ma'am,' David Morris assured her. So tenderhearted was she that Eleanor decided they would no longer watch the performance of the cruel acts.

Curiously, Eleanor sometimes took pleasure in inducing Sarah's fright. One evening, in the middle of summer, Mary-Caryll served them cabbage soup, hot bread, asparagus in butter sauce, salmon pie, and cranberry tart.

'Shall we make a circuit of the Place?' Sarah asked. She wanted to make Eleanor exercise after the heavy dinner in order to reduce the weight she was so evidently taking on. They started out along the brook to the Pengwern woods, deciding to return in time to watch the sun dip behind their chimneys and into the horizon, leaving their beloved Place in romantic rose, and then grey, shadow. As was their custom, Eleanor entertained Sarah with an anecdote from her memory as they made their way through the dying light.

'Do you remember hearing of Mrs French?'

'I don't think so.'

'An extraordinary story. She lived at Peterswell, and was, I think, a second cousin to Sir Jonah Barrington.'

'Did you know her?'

Eleanor laughed. 'When you hear this story you will be very glad I did not.'

'Continue, please,' said Sarah, watching the declining sun intently.

'Well, she was a strong-minded woman who understood the obligation of gentry to instruct the serving class in their duties. A farmer who raised sheep for a neighbouring lord had been insolent to her when she demanded a ewe of him for her table. The farmer claimed the ewe in question was his, not his master's. In an angry mood, Mrs French drove on to her orchard, where her gardener was pruning cherry trees. To him she poured out the story of the rude farmer.'

'Why? Did she have no one in her house to vent her anger to?'

'I don't know,' said Eleanor impatiently. 'She was a widow, I think.'

'I see.'

'Well, however it was, the gardener took it that he might expect preferment of some kind if he acted on behalf of his mistress. His pruning shears under his arm, he ran all the way to the field in which the farmer was tending his sheep. Coming upon the farmer from behind, he was swift to act. He clipped off his ears. The dripping appendages fell to the ground and the farmer ran screaming to his cottage. The gardener gathered up the bloody ears in his glove, carried them carefully to Mrs French's pantry, pushed

the serving maid out of the way to search for a covered
silver dish, laid them within, and then carried the dish
proudly into his mistress's parlour, where she was having
tea.'

Sarah was horrified. 'What then, my love? Did she . . . lift
the cover?'

Eleanor laughed, a cruel sound to Sarah. 'I don't know
anything more. That is all I have heard of the story.'

Sarah shuddered. The Ladies turned back towards their
house. So absorbed were they on the consequences of the
story that they wandered without noticing into a field that
was not their own. Suddenly Eleanor grabbed Sarah's hand
and began to pull her along. Over her shoulder, Sarah
spied the bull that had activated Eleanor. Nothing in the
world so frightened them as the prospect of a bull, even at
a distance. Hand in hand they clumped heavily through the
tall grass, not looking back, imagining as they went that
they felt the hot red breath of the fearsome black animal on
their necks.

They spent hours of their evenings reading. Eleanor tran-
scribed long passages into her day book. Sometimes she
practised her harp, sometimes they played backgammon
and kept their scores faithfully, although skill and luck
were bestowed equally upon them. Sarah embroidered and
wrote faithful letters to Mrs Tighe or to her father's brother,
with whom she had begun to correspond. (Passing through
Llangollen one Easter season on his way to London, he
had sent a polite inquiry about her health.) Eleanor's harp
made rough, twangy, rasping noises that Sarah claimed
she enjoyed while she painted.

Every evening before they retired, Eleanor recorded the

state of their finances. She would put money into en-
velopes for the current, small bills to be dispensed when
the creditors called at the kitchen door: 'For the Corn
Man.' 'For the Coal Man.' 'For the Butcher: our first
year's provision of pork.' Relieved that they had once
more cleared themselves in the district, she would shut the
day book and reach for Sarah's hand. Carrying their candle
and a book they would go up the stairs and come to the
room where, for them both, the most pleasurable hours of
the day would begin. It was now nine o'clock.

Settled into the New Bed, the moreen curtain drawn across
its length, Tatters and Flirt drowsing on the flourished
quilt at their feet, they are alone, within a silent house
(Mary-Caryll is permitted to retire directly after supper is
disposed of), in a vale isolated from the village: emigrants
in a foreign state, far from what they regard as the common world. Here they are royalty, goddesses, elevated and
aristocratic. They suspend all rules and relax into warm,
loving chaos. Theirs is the lenity of illicit love. They
provide their own sanctions for the singular acts they
believe they have invented. In their enormous nightcaps,
which they always wear to prevent toothache despite the
fire burning in the grate and the thick grey carpet that
warms the floor, they might appear, were they to be seen,
as figures of fun, heavy Roman generals (Titus Flavius
Sabinus Vespasianus) of the first century engaging in unlikely activities behind the heavy arras. In each other's
eyes, they are beautiful, elegant, graceful women, more
desirable than other persons in the world of either sex.
They believe they live on a higher plane and in a fuller
life, committed to a more passionate engagement than

any known to women before. They have discovered acts of
tender mutual satisfaction that reduces them to languor and
to sleep by midnight, in each other's arms, exhausted and
happy.

'Madame de Sévigné has just such a bed, I have read,'
Eleanor tells Sarah soon after theirs was erected. She does
not go on to say that she believes Madame de Sévigné,
whose letters she is reading, had a passionate love for her
daughter, Françoise, 'the prettiest girl in France,' the love-
struck mother wrote. Twenty years younger than her mother,
Françoise married a count, moved some distance away
from Paris, and broke her mother's heart.

On days of constant rain they rose later and spent their
morning before the library fire near the bookshelves they
had had built to hold their growing ('expensive') collection. On such mornings Eleanor read *La Nouvelle Héloise*
aloud, because she thought she saw in its eloquent pages a
resemblance to their own lives, while Sarah worked her
cross-stitch.

Or: Eleanor entered in her day book, made by Sarah of
mottled green boards and crimson leather spine and corners, their weekly accounts: 'shoe bill (high): £4.4s' 'candles: 6s.4p.' 'Moses Jones gardener: 10s.' 'books: 14s.3p.'
'chimney sweep: 5s.' 'cheese maker: 8s.' 'meat: 12s.'

Or: She wrote of the activities of the day past: 'My love
and I spent from 5 to 7 in the Shrubbery in the field
endeavouring to talk and walk away our little Sorrows.'
The little sorrows she does not enumerate, they being well
known to them both. Worst of them all are the migraines
that plague her monthly, so that she stays in bed for two
days, Sarah with her, bathing her forehead, purging her

with emetics and laxatives, feeding her broth and milk toast. There are Sarah's dreams and fantasies, which fail to be understood by Eleanor as real but that haunt poor Sarah for days after she has 'seen' them. There are Eleanor's continuing worries about money. Or nagging creditors. Or, for Sarah, Eleanor's increasingly bad temper. Or Sarah's fright at bulls, cliffs, the river, the impending deaths of Frisk and Hope the lamb, the rough boys on the road, the cries of babies, the poisons possibly concealed in the cheeses they are sold, being buried alive. Or Sarah's throat mucus and coughing that causes her voice, on occasion, to entirely disappear. Or Sarah's withdrawal from Eleanor that always accompanies this loss, from the traffic of the house and garden, into the silent vault of her inner self. The sorrows mount and nag, but they are always seen as 'little.' Nothing can diminish the tie that binds them, the inexplicable love they share.

When they cannot be out of doors they talk endlessly about their poverty and plot strategies to recover regular funds. They hope for Butler and Fownes generosity but are granted no sign of it. At times they allow themselves to speculate on prospective family deaths to rescue them from restraints upon their vision of life as they wish to live it, to free them from debts. Behind their talk, they hear loud, violent argument: Mary-Caryll fighting with tradesmen at the door. Once, it is with the fishmonger, who has come selling herring and oysters. The Ladies judge that the fisherman has asked too high a price for his wares. Mary-Caryll receives his quotation by beating him about the head until he lowers his price. Staunch Mary-Caryll understands well the restricted conditions under which they all live, so, acting always in their interests, she performs her loyal attacks upon those who would cheat them. As for herself, she asks no pay from her Ladies. Tradespeople fear her fists, so the day book is able to record prices lower than might be expected.

On fine days, they gardened assiduously, instructing Moses Jones how to accomplish what they envisioned. Eleanor disliked him because he often broke in upon their talk without so much as an apology and always directed his questions to Sarah, whom he thought possessed all horticultural authority about the Place. They themselves planted and weeded, trimmed and picked, working from the Plan for the garden Sarah had drawn. The grounds began to take on the aspect of decorative art: hedges, gravelled walks, the gazebo and rustic sheds and benches, statues and water font, purloined stone by stone from the courtyard of Valle Crucis, little pools and garden beds hidden in the high shrubbery, which were Sarah's greatest love.

At first they were able to hire only one gardener. Mary-Caryll had no assistance for two years. She went to the market, oiled the fine-carved oak furniture, beat and swept the rugs, and brushed and repaired her Ladies' habits and their beaver hats, which hard wear and worse weather had reduced almost to shreds. She fed the animals, built fires in every room, and heated water for their baths. Later, after the cow Margaret (named by Eleanor for her mild sister) was sent to them, she did the milking, made the butter, and sold the excess to her friend at The Hand, keeping the returns (with the Ladies' consent) for her savings. She slept well after her sixteen hours of hard labour, and grew heavier and more muscular each year.

*   *   *

Before the Ladies sleep, they fall into the habit of inserting into their ears balls of brown paper. Eleanor has heard, and now believes, that the practise will ward off deafness.

Eleanor enters into her diary an extract from Madame de Sévigné's letter to her married daughter:

> I have seated myself to write to you, at the end of this shady little walk which you love, upon a mossy bank where I have so often seen you lying. But, mon Dieu! where have I not seen you here? and how these memories grieve my heart! There is no place, no spot—either in the house or in the church, in the country or in the garden—where I have not seen you. Everything brings some memory to mind; and whatever it may be, it makes my heart ache. I see you; you are present to me. I think of everything and think again. My brain and heart grow confused. But in vain I turn—in vain I look for you: that dear child whom I passionately love is two hundred leagues distant from me. I have her no more; and then I weep and cannot cease. My love, that is weakness; but as for me, I do not know how to be strong against a feeling so powerful and so natural.

They acquire Jersey hens for whom they build a coop. They plant melon and mushroom beds, and many asparagus plants. A small stable is built by the joiner to house their cob. They put in a rose garden and holly bushes. Later, they come to think, the gardens must be both beautiful and useful. 'We will have a show place from which we can also eat,' says Eleanor, and so they proceed to build it. Now they eat very well: boiled chicken on Sun-

days as well as on Irish and Welsh holidays and feast days,
new-laid eggs, ham they have cured themselves, and mutton from village sheep because they cannot bring themselves to slaughter their own.

Sarah writes to her father's brother, Lord Bessborough: 'I
would not intrude upon your attention were it not that we
are entirely without money. Had my father survived I
cannot help but think he would not have had his daughter
in such straits.'

Against his wife's counsel, Lord Bessborough sends his
niece £150. When he dies, three years later, he leaves her
the same sum, to be granted yearly. His son attempts to
contest the bequest ('a moral objection,' he tells the court)
without success.

'*Cockroaches?* It cannot be.'

'It is indeed. Three, in the pantry, Lady Eleanor.'

Eleanor is outraged, first at Mary-Caryll for bearing the
unwelcome news, and then at the sense of invasion she
feels. Her face reddens with fury. She puts on her hat and,
saying nothing to Sarah or Mary-Caryll, starts up the road
to the village. She pounds her boots against the mossed
stones of the bridge and storms into the baker's shop.
Ignoring the waiting customers, she shouts at the baker,
informing him that vermin from his shop are marching
across the River Dee Bridge, down the Pengwern Road,
and into their Place.

*   *   *

Sarah wakes in the night, crying.

'What is it, my love?' Eleanor asks.

'I was where a joiner was hammering at pieces and ends of wood and it seemed to me he was constructing a mad house, all angles and uneven floors and short uprights. The roof would not fit the crooked posts, and you said: "Straighten it! Straighten everything," and at that moment it began to topple over, we and the joiner were buried alive under it . . .'

'A dream, my love. Now you are awake. It is over. We are on safe and steady ground, in our bed. Try to sleep again.'

Eleanor cradled Sarah in her arms. Sarah said: 'Eleanor, my love: do you still scorn the idea of God?'

'Tush, yes. That God my mother worshipped is a father I prefer not to think is real.'

'Do you not believe He made us . . . as we are? So that it is then all right to *be* as we are?'

Eleanor now understood how necessary this theological justification of their life was to Sarah. She hesitated a moment, and then she said: 'It may be so, my love. He made us as we are. We are God's superior architecture.'

Eleanor wakened at three in the morning. One side of her face throbbed painfully. She explored her mouth with her fingers and found a raw root where a tooth had been. She shook Sarah awake. Together they searched and found the tooth in the bedclothes. Eleanor moaned with pain. Sarah held her in her arms until daylight, discovering the unusual pleasure, for once, of being the comforter.

'I must go to Chester. The noon coach is to Wrexham and then from there . . .' Eleanor said. Her face was now badly swollen, her eye almost shut above the obtrusive cheek. Sarah said: 'I'll come with you.'

'No need, my love. You so dislike the coach and the bridges.'

Sarah reminded Eleanor of their vow. She did not say she was afraid of being left alone in the Place, even with Mary-Caryll 'at the back,' as they referred to the kitchen area. By nightfall they were in Chester, where, by good fortune, a Scots dentist, Mr Blair, had just arrived for a week's professional visit to the English city. While Eleanor shrieked with pain, Mr Blair extracted the stump of tooth. After she had recovered somewhat, he told her that two more of her teeth would soon crack away in the same fashion and should be removed at once.

Sarah stood beside her, holding Eleanor's hand, her eyes shut, while Mr Blair extracted the two teeth. With each extraction, Eleanor screamed, a powerful air-splitting sound, and then fainted. At the end, close to fainting herself, Sarah helped the dentist revive Eleanor with salts and comforted her while he stuffed Eleanor's mouth and bound her face with straps of tightly woven linen. Hardly able to see from pain and swelling, Eleanor leaned upon Sarah as they walked slowly to their lodgings. They spent a second sleepless night. Eleanor vomited the blood she had swallowed and groaned with pain, giving way to tears and shaking, the blood seeping from the corner of her swollen mouth.

For two days after their return to Plas Newydd, they remained in bed. On the third day Eleanor was better, although the cheek over the extraction sank into a grey hollow. They resumed their active lives. Eleanor put the terrible days out of her mind by consigning a minute description of them to the day book, where she entered the costs of the journey for them both, the stay at the inn in Oswestry, their purchases: 'Four boxes toothpowder, two brushes, recommended by Mr Blair. For these and services, gave him his demand: 3 guineas.'

They had been settled in the vale for two years when word reached them by post: Walter Butler's hereditary title had been restored. The letter was from Margaret Cavanaugh. Mr Butler was now legitimately Lord Walter Butler, Duke of Ormonde, and Eleanor's mother Lady Adelaide. The titles they had assumed unto themselves since their marriage and insisted be used by friends and servants alike, were now rightfully theirs.

'At last, I am truly a Lady,' said Eleanor. She and Sarah laughed at the belated legitimisation. They rejoiced about the one advantage it gave them: Now it was possible for Eleanor, in her 'retirement,' to apply for a pension from the government and thus add to their slender resources.

For Lord Butler it came too late. As though the restoration had overtaxed his almost blind eyes and his goutish body, the *novus homo* died in his sleep the following year. Eleanor was informed of his death by her sister in the same letter that contained the details of the funeral planned for the week next.

'I shall not go.'

'If it were I . . .'

'You would go?'

'Oh yes. As much to be in Ireland again as to pay my

respects. And I will go with you should you change your mind. And, of course, should you wish me to.'

'All very well, and thank you, but I don't intend to go. Ireland is no longer my country. Walter Butler was never a father to me. I do not mourn his passing, any more than I would one of our troublesome foxes. Less.'

'You have no feeling for him at all?'

'Yes, I confess to having one: curiosity. I am eager to know how much provision he has made for me.'

Eleanor was in bed suffering from migraine. Sarah offered to read her mail to her.

'Nothing?'

'Nothing, my love. Your sister writes that you are not mentioned at all.'

'Not mentioned,' Eleanor said, as though the phrase were an incantation uttered to produce income by magical repetition. 'Not mentioned at all.'

'But your sister adds that Morton Cavanaugh is prepared to make provision for you, two hundred pounds yearly, from their share of the estate. The great bulk of it, she says, is of course left to your mother. But upon her death the title and the castle devolve upon Margaret and Morton's son, Walter, now aged eighteen months.'

'I had no knowledge of a nephew,' Eleanor said wearily. She reversed the cloth that covered her eyes.

Eleanor replied to her mother at Kilkenny and to her sister at Borris, with the same letter, angrily protesting the will: 'I will appeal to the English crown for a suitable settlement. Then it will be seen by the whole world how barbarously I have been treated.'

*   *   *

So it is: The longer they live together the more the Ladies think of themselves as victims, not agents, of their bold act. They are convinced they have been cruelly misunderstood by their families. Theirs is the innocence of invention and discovery. They believe they deserve support befitting their station and praise for the uniqueness of their courageous excursion into a new human continent: They are explorers who have scaled unknown peaks. In demanding support, they wish their families, even their country, to reward their ambition and their bravery.

Eleanor computes in her day book while Sarah sketches Flirt, asleep on the love seat: '£180—Mrs Tighe. £150—from the Lord Bessborough estate. £150—my sister. Until our pensions are granted,' she writes, 'we can just nearly make do. The tradesmen in the district are trusting.'

'We might of course buy fewer books,' Sarah says.

Eleanor looks at her unbelievingly and says nothing.

'Less meat?' Sarah ventures.

Eleanor's appetite has grown with her girth. She eats twice as much as Sarah, so she sees this suggestion as a gentle reprimand. She makes no reply. Sarah then says quickly: 'Oh my love, yes. We shall easily make do.'

So their lives advance, secluded, serene, secret, and, to them, exceptional. They address each other always by the sentimental appellations they used in their earliest love. Eleanor's day book continues to keep note of sugary small daily events: 'My beloved and I in sweet repose,' she writes.

'My beloved and I walked to Balen Baeche . . . there found a very pretty young woman spinning,' she writes.

'My beloved and I went a delicious walk round Edward Evans's field,' she writes, and 'The delight of my heart and I spent a day of strict retirement, sentiment, and delight.'

Sarah keeps no record of her life and thoughts. She trusts Eleanor's accounting, knowing it is far better arithmetic than she could do. She prefers her pictures, her elegant embroidery work, the books she binds and decorates. She reads the day book and frowns at the generalisations with which Eleanor covers their moments of passion. Had she her way they would not be recorded at all.

But Eleanor never thinks of discretion. She has no concern for the reaction of anyone who happens upon the record when they are both gone. Posterity will admire their careful notation of the money strictly meted out to them and spent so recklessly. The word 'sentiment,' she writes often, and 'sentiment and delight.' With that phrase she covers the fusions of their days and nights, the linking of hands and mouths, the coupling of warm arms, every pleasure of their bodies, and their now free spirits.

In the first years their company was limited to each other, the gardener, and to the domestics, farm animals, and, always, the faithful Mary-Caryll, more friend than servant. Later, they acquired a second gardener, a maid for chamber work, and another for scullery; those young girls came to them each day from the village, and so the Place often seemed to the Ladies too full of people. Eleanor had many disagreements with the servants and gardeners, during which she lost her temper and called them all manner of names reflecting upon their mental capacities and their family origins. One after another, they left the Ladies' employ.

A small altercation between a hireling and Eleanor created a near revolution in the town. A boy taken on by the gardener to help with some repairs to the pond came late to work one morning. This defection from strict duty might have gone unnoticed had Eleanor not had a bad night due to the midnight onset of a migraine headache. Standing at her window at half after eight, her burning forehead pressed against the cold pane, and waiting for Sarah to wake and tend to her, she saw the boy racing towards the dairy, bent over against the hedge to avoid, she was certain, being seen during his criminally late arrival. For days, while she recovered from her affliction, she pondered a fit punishment for the tardy lad. She sought him out while he was shovelling out the dairy.

'You were late, very late on Monday,' she said to the boy.

'Monday you say, ma'am? Oh ya, Monday. Well Monday me maw had me baby brother and I waited to see,' he said in a low, ashamed voice.

'So,' said Eleanor. 'Now it will be necessary to come at five, not seven-thirty as you have been. Margaret needs her feed earlier, I believe.' Eleanor felt safe in this decree, knowing the family now had a new mouth to feed and the boy's employment was necessary.

Indignation filled the boy's family when he reported Lady Eleanor's dictum, and spread to the neighbours. It was decided to send a delegation to Plas Newydd to protest. The argument was that the boy's maw had need of the lad in the early morning to see to the younger ones.

Eleanor would not come to the door to meet the group of townspeople when Mary-Caryll brought word of their arrival. Sarah said she would go.

'No,' said Eleanor firmly. 'They do not deserve a hearing. This is absurd.'

'Yes,' said Sarah firmly, for once.

Sarah's soft voice and gentle manner persuaded the delegation that perhaps five was a bit early for the domestic affairs of the boy's family but that six-thirty was a good time for Margaret's breakfast. The group departed content.

Soon after the visitation Sarah took over the management of the household, and Eleanor retired to her studies and her books. They began to read more widely, Tasso, Ariosto, and other medieval Italian writers, the Latin classics in English translations, Ossian, William Cowper, Dr. Johnson. They enjoyed travel books and collections of French letters, books about formal gardens, animal husbandry, the novels of Jean-Jacques Rousseau, Samuel Richardson, and Henry Fielding. In everything they read, they searched for literary confirmation of their own natures, evidence of the existence of women like themselves. Their desire was not so much to find allies as to identify themselves as belonging properly in some corner, at the point of some acute angle in the geometry of the human race. In the evenings, with all the windows closed and the shutters secured against the ambiguities and terrors of the night outside, a clutch of candles lit close to their book, they scoured the pages for some mention of an existence like their own.

*   *   *

Harriet Bowdler, whose unacknowledged notions had been fired by the sight of the two good companions seemingly welded into a single unit by the bonds of love and friendship, wrote to Sarah, the one she deemed most amenable to correspondence. She received a most civil reply. Sarah's letter suggested to Harriet that she would relish receiving mail, and so began a constant exchange of letters. Harriet had placed herself in readiness, she told Sarah, to receive an invitation to visit Plas Newydd. None was offered, so she compensated for the lapse by inventing a gay and lively social life of her own in Oswestry with which she filled the pages of her letters, one each week. Sarah, for her part, kept her abreast of the small household details of life at the New Place. Every planting was given a paragraph, every building full description; often she made a small illustration to accompany the prose. But never did she ask Harriet Bowdler to visit: 'We do not go about beyond the village. We have no visitors,' she wrote to the avid Harriet.

Canny Harriet read the letter about the newly erected dairy and decided on a way to bring herself, eventually, into the Ladies' company. When she heard that the last nail had been driven into the building 'which now is ample for a single beast,' she wrote to Sarah:

'For long I have wanted to send something to make your Shrine to Friendship, as I think of it, more sufficient unto itself. With a farmer whose cart is being driven to Llangollen to bring back hay I have sent to you and Lady Eleanor a milk cow.'

Margaret the cow quickly became a well-loved member of the household. In the evenings the Ladies took a lantern and walked a quarter of the Home Circuit to visit their 'dear Margaret,' as Eleanor described her in the day book.

Her mournful, polished-brown eyes appealed to their romantic souls. They petted and smoothed her suede back; she in turn bestowed her flat, red tongue upon their palms, a gesture they interpreted as a sign of bovine affection. They were delighted at the gift. They had acquired a new friend.

Rarely did they purchase 'modern books,' Eleanor's term for anything issued by the presses after the year 1750. But they had heard of one Thomas Pennant, an inveterate traveller who had published an account of his tours of Wales a few years before. The Ladies sent to England for the book, and Eleanor began to read it aloud in the evening, pleased to be able to retrace their own footsteps while they sat comfortably in their library.

'She was an unusual woman,' Eleanor said. She fell silent while Sarah searched under her chair for her dropped needle.

'Who?'

'Margaret uch Evan. Thomas Pennant writes of her.'

'Read to me about her.'

' "She is at this time about ninety years of age—" '

'Ninety?'

'Ninety. "She was Wales's greatest hunter, shooter, and fisher of her time." Do you imagine he means when she was younger by "of her time" or when she was ninety?'

'Go on. Perhaps he will say.'

'Such imprecision is very tiresome.'

'Go on, love.'

' "She kept a dozen at least of dogs, terriers, greyhounds and spaniels, all excellent in their kinds. She killed

more foxes, in one year, than all the confederate hunts do
in ten; rowed stoutly and was queen of the lake—" '

'Queen of the lake. What lake? Where did she live?'

'Penllyn, he says.'

'Where is that?'

'I have no idea. He goes on: "She fiddled excellently,
and knew all our old music; did not neglect the mechanic
arts, for she was a very good joiner—" '

'That too. He does not say that she played the harp?'

Eleanor laughed. 'No, but he does report that she *made*
harps. Also, she shoed her own horses and made her own
shoes as well.'

Sarah laughed. 'We would do well to learn *that* art.'

'Oh, indeed we would.'

'Read on.'

' "Margaret was also blacksmith, shoemaker, boat
builder." That seems to be because she had a contract to
convey copper ore down the lakes in her own boats.'

'What lakes?'

'He does not specify.'

'Go on.'

' "All the neighbouring bards paid their addresses to
Margaret, and celebrated her exploits in pure British verse." '

'How wonderful! To be celebrated in verse. I suppose
she never married?'

'Why do you say that?'

'She must have been so accomplished, so . . . so sufficient to herself that she would not have required the support of a husband.'

'That might have been true. Nevertheless, she married,
very late it seems. Mr Pennant says: "At length"—which
is hardly informative, is it?—"at length she gave her hand
to the most effeminate of her admirers as if predetermined

to maintain the superiority which Nature had bestowed on her." '

They sat in silence, contemplating Thomas Pennant's narrative.

Then Sarah asked: ' "The most effeminate of her admirers?" Does that mean that manly Margaret uch Evan married a ladylike man?'

'Apparently so.'

'Perhaps he *was* a woman?'

'Perhaps.'

'And was she really a man wearing the clothing of a woman, do you suppose?'

'Why should we suppose that? She was extraordinary because she combined womanliness with masculine accomplishments. Does that make her a man—or more a woman?'

Sarah was unable to reply to Eleanor's question. She was in tears.

'Oh my dear. What *is* it?' Eleanor did not wait for an answer, indeed expected none. Sarah's crying spells had mysterious origins, rising out of the ground or from the shadows like the fair folk Twlwyth Teg. They lasted only a short time, and then dissipated into apology and regret. Never was she sure, yet Eleanor postulated the causes from her experience of them: sexual matters, especially those that contained confusion of sexes, reduced Sarah to tears. Animal suffering, dead birds and chipmunks and field mice. Eleanor's pain. Religious discussions. Unpleasantness of any sort in the household. The appearance of a hole at the bottom of a boot or walking shoe. Thoughts of death. Eleanor kept a silent, annotated catalogue of such subjects so that she might recognize a new cause when it appeared or be prepared for the inevitable results of the old causes.

To turn her away from her undefined sorrow, Eleanor asked Sarah: 'Shall we think of our cow as named for Margaret uch Evan instead of for my sister? Surely she is more stalwart than that whey-faced fool?'

Sarah wiped her eyes and smiled.

'I agree our dear Margaret is a fitting namesake for Thomas Pennant's heroine. Do you suppose Margaret uch Evan is still alive?'

'I am sure she is. Like Cassandra or Medea or Deidre, she belongs to mythology, not history. She will always be alive.'

'I regret she is said to have killed so many foxes.'

'Oh yes, the foxes. Is that what made you sad?'

'No. It was for us. I cried for us.'

'For *us*, my love?'

'For our . . . our . . . Oh, I don't know quite. For all the confusion. Hers. Her lady-husband's. Ours. All of it.'

'I see.' But Eleanor did not. What was clear to her was Sarah's deep and clouded confusion. In Eleanor's passion for Sarah the sun shone always, in great clarity. To Sarah's mind, grey mist and fog covered the landscape and obscured her inner vision.

Margaret Cavanaugh writes to her sister: 'Our mother is very weak. Her doctors despair of her life. Yesterday when I came she said she w^d have written to you in these last years but you had never sent an address to her. Can this be true? She believes you left with Miss Ponsonby last week when of course we know it is years since your precipitous departure. Still she grieves for the scandal over the whole countryside that dismay[d] us all so greatly. I ask[d] if she wish[d] to see you, if you sh[d] come to Kilkenny. She gave no answer. It is for you to decide if you wish to come to receive her Last Blessing.'

Eleanor writes: 'No. I do not wish to come.'

It is September 1793: Three weeks after the first letter, Margaret Cavanaugh writes again to her sister: 'She did not ask for you before her death which was slow but peaceful and occurr[d] at noon yesterday. We were at her bedside and the servants, attending her for nine days and many of the nights. The will is to be open[d] to us when her agents come to Borris week next. For we must be off to home after the funeral to see to Our Walter's departure for St. Anselm's. Our Mother will be buried beside Our Father tomorrow eleven, after a Requiem High Mass.

'Ellen is worried about employment in a good place and asks if there is a place with you for her. To you privately I say I think her too old to be of much service to anyone. Milligan will come to us as cellarman. Butlering is now too heavy for him but he is a good worker.'

Eleanor and Sarah wait anxiously for word that Lady Adelaide's will has been read. When it comes, it is that Eleanor is not mentioned in the will. It is a blow, but they have been buffeted by fiscal disappointments before. There is still no word from official lists of their pensions. This too they accept stoically.

Eleanor enters in her day book: 'Lady Adelaide died September the twelfth. I cannot care.'

To Sarah she says: 'I never loved her. I should have expected nothing from her.' And then after a moment she adds: 'And I believe she never loved me.'

*   *   *

Mary-Caryll was busy all the summer. In her spare time each day, she dug potatoes and sold them at the weekly village fair for £1, 10s. With the Ladies' permission she put the sum away with her savings.

Until the time when they agreed to admit visitors to their Place, into their shrubbery, to their dining table and library, their entire attention was focussed on the beautification of Plas Newydd, on themselves and the 'improvement' of their minds, and on their dear animals. For Eleanor the livestock and domestic pets were adjuncts to her feudal view of the Place, but to Sarah they were children, to be petted and cossetted. Their first true visitor was an animal. For, before the barrier for persons was lowered, in the late fall and after two years of 'retirement,' the Ladies heard from Mary-Caryll that a trained bear was being exhibited in the village. Sarah's excitement was very great. After their breakfast saucer of tea she carried their plates to Mary-Caryll in the kitchen.

'Will you stop at The Hand today and ask Mr Lewis to accompany you here?'

'For sure. He likes to be asked.'

Mr Lewis was Mrs Edmunds's handwright and general factotum. He was a genial, hardworking widower who enjoyed watching over his employer's infant son almost as much as horse grooming, bartending, or making repairs to the rooms and public areas of The Hand. 'Mrs Edmunds is very hard on rest and free time from labour,' he reported to the Ladies, so he was always pleased to be sent for to drive them in the chaise about the countryside or to do small repairs to their house.

'We have heard of the bear,' Eleanor told Mr Lewis when he came with Mary-Caryll.

'Yes, m'lady. It is a sight to see.'

'Could you ask its owner to bring it here to us this evening?'

'Indeed I could.'

Eleanor paid him and gave him extra money to pay the bear's owner. The Ladies waited impatiently until late afternoon, when Mary-Caryll alerted them to the approach. They went to the gate to witness the slow progress towards them of a giant of a man wearing a bright red cap, a green shirt, and plaid trousers. By a chain he led a huge brown bear. As it marched stolidly along, the bear's coat swayed from side to side in the evening wind. It was ponderous and weary-looking.

The man introduced himself to the Ladies as Master Dan.

'And this is Nancy.'

At the sound of her name, the bear rose on her rear legs, snorted, and lifted her flat brown snout into the air. Her underbelly exposed shrivelled tits and short white hair. Then she lowered her paws to the Ladies' feet. Sarah was enthralled.

'May we feed Nancy?' Sarah asked.

'Yes mum. She eats everlastingly. Meats, nuts, porridge, ever thin.'

Sarah almost ran to the house and returned quickly with a plate piled with slices of mutton and bread.

'Bread too she likes,' said Master Dan after he saw the plate. 'But never potatoes.'

'Why so?'

'Tastes, mum. Nancy has tastes like ever one.'

'What does she drink?'

Master Dan smiled. 'Beer.'

'Beer?'

'Beer, yes mum. Taste, like ever one else.'

Eleanor shook her head but went off to the brewing kitchen, a new addition to the Place since the summer.

Sarah watched Nancy closely. She was huge and tame, at once affectionate and forbidding. Her size alone was fearsome, but the soft appearance of her fur invited human touch. Sarah was unable to resist. When Eleanor returned with a large pewter bowl filled with their own brewed small beer she found Nancy standing almost erect and Sarah in the bear's embrace, the upper half of Sarah's body hidden in Nancy's thick hairy arms. Eleanor put the bowl down hastily.

'Sarah, come away.'

Nancy, who had sniffed the beer, disengaged herself and came down almost on top of Sarah in her eagerness to drink. Eleanor moved Sarah clear of the great paws. Master Dan looked relieved.

'She is tame, mum. But I donna she'd take to hugs en kisses en such.'

Sarah blushed and moved back. From a little distance she watched Nancy drinking in enormous gulps. In seconds the beer was gone. Nancy lifted her head and swung it around to look at Sarah.

'She knows me,' said Sarah. 'She wants more beer.'

'No, mum. No more. She has enough now to dance. I'll show you.'

Master Dan led the bear to the middle of the field before the house and took the chain from her neck. He gave her a command. The bear proceeded slowly through a series of tricks: walking on two feet while erect, in one direction and then the other, rolling like a great tun on her back while waving her paws in the air, running in a wide, lumbering circle around her master, and then, as a finale, allowing him to ride astride her back, holding on to her coat as she ran without pattern around the field trying playfully to shake her rider, but enduring him nonetheless.

Master Dan reattached the chain and led Nancy to the Ladies.

Sarah looked troubled. 'Is she always kept chained when she is not performing?'

'Oh yes, mum. It's village ordnance.'

'I see. But even so tame an animal?'

'Yes, mum. None trusts bears. They don't know um. But Nan has got angry, and does swipe out.'

Eleanor, seeing the signs of approaching sorrow in Sarah, quickly picked up the bowl. 'We thank you for coming. We enjoyed the exhibition.'

'She'll be on the green to week's end should you want to see her once more,' said Master Dan, tipping his cap and tugging on Nancy's chain to urge her along with him.

Nancy stood still, her round brown eyes fixed on Sarah. There was a long, heavy moment, like a tableau, while Eleanor looked at Sarah with concern, Master Dan at Nancy, and Nancy stared yearningly, it appeared, at Sarah.

'She likes me, I believe,' said Sarah to the air. No one replied. Nancy took two heavy steps forward, but Master Dan pulled her back.

'Come on, gal. We're to home.'

'Once more, thank you,' Eleanor said. She put her arm around Sarah, knowing before she looked at her face that it would be wet with tears.

For days afterwards they talked of the bear. Sarah wanted

to walk into the village to see her again but Eleanor would not agree. Of course Sarah did not go without her. When next they took their excursion to Llangollen, Nancy and her Master Dan were gone.

Eleanor noted the bear's visit in her day book: 'Our first visitor to the front gate.' For her the matter ended there. Sarah continued to think of Nancy, to dream of her. Once she woke in fright, having seen a coffin containing a dead child with a bear arm and claw to which Sarah found herself attaching a string and bell. Nancy became a character in her fantasies. She remembered her long, loving look, as she believed it to have been. She wondered if it was possible that the bear, despite her heavy brown coat and formidable paws, was—like them.

THE
VISITORS

It *may* *have* *been* *the* *bear* *that* *broke* *the* *barrier.* *No* longer were all visitors kept from their Place. It may be, too, that the Ladies had grown tired of each other's exclusive company. Or even, that the long honeymoon was finally ended and the ordinary days, like those in a marriage, stretched out before them, at times in need of some filling.

After the years of isolation, their first human guest was Harriet Bowdler.

The mail brought in post bags from Oswestry contained a letter from Miss Bowdler. She had now devised a new stratagem. She wrote, as always, to Sarah:

'I am to Dublin next month. May I come to y^r door to see y^r dear face once more?'

'What shall I reply?'

'If you wish, tell her to come.'

'And you, my love?'

'She expresses no desire to see *my* dear face, so her presence will hardly involve me.'

'Oh love, think of the pleasure and the sweet butter her gift has given us.'

'Very true. I will be civil on dear Margaret's account. Instruct Miss Bowdler to stop at The Hand, and we will walk to her and return here for dinner. Inform her we always dine at three.'

'Shall we offer her the State Bedchamber for the night? The coach for Holyhead I believe is very early in the morning.'

There was a long silence. 'Let us see how dinner progresses this time. The night visit can wait for another.'

Harriet was the perfect encomiast. She expressed herself as enthralled with everything she saw. With the Ladies in attendance to point to their particular, favourite places, she made the Home Circuit. She paid her respects to Margaret, reminding her of her origins, and, from afar, to the sheep. She applauded the romantic aura of the plantings, the stone fonts and fountains and benches, the excellence of the library. She was especially admiring of the State Bedchamber, lingering there to notice the colours, the fine plump palliasse on the bed, the carved-oak wall decorations. Eleanor was downstairs pouring their before-dinner sherry. Sarah, faithful to instructions, did not extend their hospitality for the night's stay in the much-praised bedroom.

Dinner conversation was stiff and awkward, as though the Ladies in their seclusion had forgotten how to apply the unguents of small talk and gossip to an occasion involving a guest. For her part, Harriet was bewildered by the names of the authors they had read and of whom she had not heard. For their part, the Ladies appeared to be uninterested in Oswestry goings-on. Eleanor, who commanded the dinner table in a manner reminiscent of Lord Walter, made one concession to conviviality. She observed that the butter they were applying to their bread was freshly made yesterday from Harriet's gift, their dear Margaret. This pleased Harriet, who then proceeded to narrate the long saga of the breeding, feeding, choosing, purchase, and transportation of Margaret.

Eleanor's mood darkened as the visit lengthened. Breaking in upon Harriet's bovine tale, she observed that the morning coach was at seven and would not stop at the head of their road so that Harriet had better make a start for the village.

'It has been wonderful,' Harriet said to Sarah at the door, pressing her hand. Eleanor had remained seated at the table after bidding Harriet a cool goodbye.

'I am so glad.'

'I cannot wait to see you again. And you must remember to call upon me at Oswestry.'

'We do not go abroad at all,' said Sarah, looking back at Eleanor. Her glance seemed to suggest the particular aversion that Eleanor had to returning visits. Sarah walked with Harriet to their gate to bid her goodbye again. Impulsively, Harriet leaned to kiss Sarah on the cheek, and then again pressed her hand.

'Thank you. Thank you, my dear,' said Harriet before she went up the road, thinking, as she walked, of the Sarah she had just left, dressed in her strange outfit, her starched neckcloth, her cropped hair heavily powdered, her dear face.

They could not have foreseen that Harriet's enthusiasm for their 'sweet repose,' as she described it to her friends, would occupy all her conversation for weeks to come. Despite the hardships of communication, bad roads, infrequent post, word about the Ladies, their beautiful garden and shrubberies and most of all, the curiosities they themselves appeared to be, was transmitted from her in all directions. Stories about 'the fair recluses' spread throughout the countryside, were conveyed by travellers on the stage coach to London, survived the stormy waters and shaky packet to Dublin to travel south to Kilkenny, to Woodstock, indeed the length of the country to Waterford, following the full round of the Ladies' own fateful journey years before. Everyone heard of their odd ménage, and speculated about it. Many spoke of them as a deserving oddity, worthy of a stop on a journey to London, like Mt. Snowden and Valle Crucis. Aristocratic hunters who came in their own chaises from England to North Wales for the fine grouse moors, the pheasant, and the rough shooting for snipe and partridge, as well as fishermen who sought salmon in the Dee, walked the Ladies' road as far as the gate, but came no closer to the two curiosities they had hoped to see. Sarah was horrified at the sight of hunters. She closed the shutters when she saw them approaching, their 'shoots' (as she called them) on their shoulders. She had devised many thickets in the low, rough spots of their Place to protect game birds against poachers and hunters.

Eleanor wrote: 'Sometimes I believe my Beloved sympathizes so with hunted beasts and fowls because she considers them related to us in situation and spirit. Plas Newydd is a thicket, affording cover for us, two Lady birds.'

*   *   *

Visits started slowly, with polite notes penned to the Ladies for permission to view what the writer had heard were 'sublime Shrubberies.' To all such requests Eleanor wrote a cold refusal. The new vow they had taken together, framed by Eleanor, and seconded meekly by Sarah, was 'no creature without names and certainly not without manners' would be permitted entry to their grounds or the house.

To the discomfort of the English aristocracy, who were known to enjoy the spectacle of peculiarity, Eleanor became almost savage, selecting among them only those she considered to be *visites distinguées*. If the name was not of highest title, or the letters were in the least demanding, or assuming and lordly, she denied the writer admission. Her temper was turned upon those who applied without acceptable crest and seal. It became even fiercer when the Civil List was published, containing the Ladies' names and the amounts of their grants: twelve pounds the quarter, each of them. Their expectations had been far higher.

Eleanor attributed the paltry amounts to revenge by the Secretary, Lord Steele, who was related to her family. Sarah suggested in a low voice: 'It may be due to our unusual way of life which is counter to others on the Pensions List.' This suggestion sent Eleanor into fresh fury. She went upstairs to a small room off the master bedroom where she often hung her aeolian harp before the open window. Under the influence of its toneless twangings, she brooded about injustice and their poverty.

The second visitor 'from the world outside' was a Mr Edmund Burke. The gentleman wrote to say he was travelling to Dublin in April and would be most honoured if he

were permitted to see their 'much-praised legendary surroundings.' He reminded the Ladies of his 'place,' The
Gregories, and stated he would be eager to learn from their
experiences with Plas Newydd some of the secrets of their
evident success. His letter accompanied a pamphlet he had
written about his opinions on the peoples' revolt in France.
Before the Ladies responded, they read his *Reflections on
the French Revolution*.

'In every respect he is right,' said Eleanor. In this
proclamation Sarah understood that Eleanor meant that his
anti-gallicism matched hers to her satisfaction.

'Burke. Burke,' Eleanor continued. 'He must have been
Dublin-born. I wonder what his thoughts are on the troublesome Irish rights question. Well. No matter. Shall we
invite him to stop?'

Mr Burke was all that Eleanor hoped he would be: charming, witty, eloquent, aristocratic in his tastes and manners.
He was a little older than Eleanor, the Ladies guessed, but
he had retained his youthful looks and figure. He had been
travelling with his school friend, Richard Shackleton. Burke
was prudent; he did not bring his friend unannounced to
luncheon but walked to Plas Newydd to ask permission, a
procedural delicacy Eleanor found both proper and endearing. Then he walked back to the Lion to fetch his friend.

Luncheon was a success. Burke praised the cheese and
the peppered ham. Richard Shackleton was enthusiastic
about the fresh fruit and clotted cream. Sarah explained the
sweetness of the plums and peaches as a function of the
fan-shaped trees she had trained, permitting the fruit full
exposure to the sun. Mr Burke admired her ingenuity in
shaping the trees to a purpose and asked for instructions on

how to do the same at The Gregories. They both expressed astonishment at how Sarah achieved a 'wild quality' with her cultivated gardens. She acknowledged she had been aided in the accomplishment of her 'effects' by Eleanor's willingness to rent land for her new arrangements on both sides of the Cuffleymen, the little brook that ran along the bottom of their land. From the east side of their house they had planted an avenue of birches leading to the brook, over which Mr Lewis had constructed a rustic bridge. Sarah explained proudly that in return for two kegs of their home-brewed beer, some strong villagers had moved large, well-shaped stones into place on each bank, in an organised arrangement dictated by Sarah's meticulously drawn plan. Mr Jones had piped water from the brook to allow it to trickle slowly over the stones. Now dark green moss and light, airy ferns grew on the banks among the stones. Sarah called these growths 'romantic accretions.' In every direction the vistas created were picturesque, as Mr Burke graciously remarked.

Mr Burke and Mr Shackleton were impressed beyond words, they said, with everything they saw. Eleanor was so taken with Mr Burke that she did not rush the two men away, as Sarah had expected. They all sat into the evening on a knoll bordered with rose bushes, at the center of which the brook made its exuberant way over the rough stones.

'How many kinds of roses do you have, would you say?' asked Mr Burke of Sarah.

'Forty-four, I think it was, last time we counted. We send everywhere for them. And of course we buy the bushes directly if we are fortunate enough to find them at the fairs.'

They talked on about their Place and about Mr Burke's,

about the art of creating corners of evocative sentimentality by embedding funeral urns and obelisks into beds of Snowden pinks and gentianella. Sarah was emboldened to explain her future plans: to hang on their trees pithy and instructive—even elevating—sayings in Italian, French, and German as well as in English and Welsh. After they had all suggested appropriate epigrams the conversation turned to politics. Mr Burke expanded upon his pamphlet. Unanimous agreement was expressed with his views. Seated among the carefully plotted artificialities of the Ladies' gardens, they talked of the effect of the beauties of the natural world upon the integrity and health of the soul. Happily separated from the rough world of the village, the county of Cymru and its rude inhabitants, they spoke of achieving an air of cultivated and thoughtful melancholy for their landscape.

The conversation turned to matters of reading. The Ladies spoke of their admiration for Jean-Jacques Rousseau's novel, which they were now re-reading. Mr Burke expanded upon Marcus Tullius Cicero:

'At Trinity I read Cicero for the first time. He has had the greatest influence upon my life. I vowed to myself that I would model my behaviour upon his example. I would try to achieve his eloquence, his high ethical standards, his philosophy, indeed, his very character.'

For once, Eleanor was almost dumb with admiration. 'How noble and how useful, to have chosen a model so early in life! Did you attempt to emulate Cicero's prose as well?'

Mr Burke laughed. 'I would have, I'm sure, had I felt adequate to so elevated an example. No, I find now I most admire the essays of Joseph Addison. I should be honoured to be counted among his literary followers.'

Eleanor made a mental note to send for a volume of Joseph Addison's essays.

In the afternoon of a fine day in late spring, 1790, the yipping of their dogs and the loud mooing of Margaret drew the Ladies to a part of the garden they reserved for 'pensive sitting,' as Eleanor termed it in the day book. On their usual resting bench sat a young man writing in a notebook. Flirt ran in circles around his legs, barking wildly. The young man looked up, startled by the Ladies' sudden appearance. They looked as he had been told they would, two aging women in riding habits and high hats. Their bushy hair was cropped short and snowy white with powder. Yet, in person, they looked more absurd than he had been led to expect.

'Who may you be?' Eleanor asked imperiously. Sarah stood close, her hand resting on Eleanor's arm, frightened as she always was before strange men, but determined not to leave Eleanor unprotected.

'I am Ian Corwin, correspondent to the *General Evening Post*. I am sent to write a report about your excellent gardens.'

At this announcement of intention Sarah was inclined to relent. But Eleanor stood still, rigid with anger.

'You have not been invited here. Leave at once.'

The young man smiled cheerfully. He stood up and extended his hand to Eleanor. She paid no heed and turned her back on the correspondent, slapping her crop ominously against her leg. The Ladies left together, entered their front door, and locked it behind them. Trained to take advantage of opportunity, the young man followed them at a distance, and when they had entered the house, peered into a library window. Through one of the few clear panes he saw Lady Eleanor stride through the hall and toss her hat at a peg 'with the air of a sportsman,' as he was to write. Sarah Ponsonby was not in his sight. But in a moment, as he stood fascinated, inspecting what he could see of the ornate furniture and the numerous books on the wall shelves, she appeared, accompanied by a huge, forceful-looking woman who carried a heavy walking stick.

Mr Corwin retreated quickly, tripping over a yew bush planted close to the house. Mary-Caryll appeared at the front door. The journalist took one look at Molly the Bruiser and ran as fast as he could. He took the gate with a leap and ran until he was out of sight of the house. Only when he stopped to dust off his trousers did he find that he had dropped his notebook under the window, probably among the damned bushes, he thought.

'Oh well, no matter,' he told himself. 'I'll remember what I've seen. To be sure, I'll never be able to forget it.'

A fortnight later the *General Evening Post* in its second page, entitled 'The Home,' published his story. The headline was EXTRAORDINARY FEMALE AFFECTION and the subtitle read *Lady Hermits:*

Miss Butler and Miss Ponsonby have retired from society into a certain Welsh Vale.

Both Ladies are daughters of the great Irish families whose names they retain.

Miss Butler, who is of the Ormonde family, had several offers of marriage, all of which she rejected. Miss Ponsonby, her particular friend and companion, was supposed to be the bar to all matrimonial union. It was thought proper to separate them, and Miss Butler was confined.

The two Ladies, however, found means to elope together. But being soon overtaken, they were each brought back by their respective relations. Many attempts were renewed to draw Miss Butler into marriage. But upon her solemnly and repeatedly declaring that nothing could induce her to wed any one, her parents ceased to persecute her by any more offers.

Not many months after, the Ladies concerted and executed a fresh elopement. Each having a small sum with them, and having been allowed a trifling income, the place of their retreat was confided to a female servant of the Butler family, who was sworn to secrecy as to the place of their retirement. She was only to say that they were well and safe and hoped that their friends would without further enquiry, continue their annuities, which has not only been done but increased.

The beautiful above-mentioned vale is the spot they fixed on where they have resided for several years unknown to the neighbouring villagers by any other appellation than the Ladies of the Vale!

Miss Butler is tall and masculine. She wears always a riding habit, hangs her hat with the air of a sportsman in the hall, and appears in all respects as a man, if we except the petticoats which she still retains.

Miss Ponsonby, on the contrary, is polite and effeminate, fair and beautiful. In Mr Secretary Steele's list of Pensions for 1788, there are the names of Elinor Butler and Sarah Ponsonby, for annuities of fifty pounds each. We have many reasons to imagine that these pensioners are the Ladies of the Vale; their female confidante continues to send them their Irish annuities beside.

They live in neatness, elegance and taste. Two females are their only servants.

Miss Ponsonby does the duties and honours of the house, while Miss Butler superintends the gardens and the rest of the grounds.

Always alert to opportunities for correspondence, Harriet Bowdler sent the Ladies the newspaper clipping for July 20, 1790, containing Ian Corwin's report, together with her usual placatory comments. But the paper had already arrived at Plas Newydd by subscription. This time Eleanor did not read the piece aloud but passed it to Sarah without comment. Sarah read it, waiting for the explosion she knew surely would come from Eleanor.

'Replete with lies and innuendo. The fool cannot even spell my name correctly.'

'Don't be angry, my love. No one will read or bother with such claptrap.'

'*No* one? *Every*one will read it and believe it. We will be overrun with curiosity-seekers come to see the freakish women of "extraordinary affection." They will tramp about in our garden like . . . like vermin, like the baker's cockroaches.'

Eleanor sat down to her desk and wrote with many angry flourishes for a few moments. She cancelled their subscription to the *Post* 'for essential reasons,' as she put it.

She wrote a second letter to their new acquaintance, Edmund Burke: 'My dear Sir: Tell us, please, by return post, how we may clear our reputations of these calumnies. Think of our families' feelings on reading these innuendos. What will those who are charged with forming the Pensions List believe of us? Can this wretched writer, who intruded upon our property and our privity, be brought to law? If we should instigate a legal action, would this be a costly procedure for us?'

Sarah read the two letters and made no comment. She handed them back to Eleanor, whose eyes, she noticed, were now half shut. Eleanor pressed her temples with her fists. Sarah recognised the signs of approaching migraine and knew it was now hopeless to prevent the sick unpleasantness of the next few days. She sighed deeply.

'Why do you sigh? Is there something not right in the letter to Mr Burke?'

'I am wondering . . . If we bring the newspaper to book for printing this . . . this story, will we not be drawing further attention to ourselves?'

Eleanor coughed, a deep catarrhal rumble sounding in her throat. She started towards the stairs.

'My head is very bad, my dearest. I must go to bed.'

Sarah sighed again, this time suppressing the sound. 'I will come with you.'

Having made Eleanor as comfortable as she could, setting her nightcap securely about her ears, placing a cool cloth across her forehead and eyes, and darkening the room, Sarah came into the bed beside her and placed her arm gently under Eleanor's neck. Eleanor did not stir. She seemed paralysed and blinded with pain.

'My beloved,' said Sarah, almost in a whisper. 'It is not a matter of great moment. But before we think of appearing before an English court, should we not consider . . .'

Sarah hesitated. Eleanor could not summon the strength to question her.

'Consider that while we wish it had not been said in the paper . . .'

Eleanor grunted, a deep anonymous sound.

Sarah went on softly: 'Even so, my love, most of it . . . .' Again she hesitated. Eleanor made a low throat sound and then coughed. Sarah reached for the pewter bowl and held it close to Eleanor's mouth as she vomited into it. Despite Eleanor's pressing physical needs, and even despite the evident pain she was in, Sarah felt compelled to continue.

'Most of it . . . is true.'

She waited for Eleanor's wrath. She could not see her

eyes under the cloth. She watched her heavy, soft breasts moving beneath her night dress. There was no sound except for Eleanor's laboured breathing. She was asleep. Sarah went on speaking to herself: ' "Extraordinary Female Affection." "Her particular friend and companion, Miss Ponsonby." "A fresh elopement." ' Then she smiled, remembering 'fair and beautiful.' Moving closer, she stretched her body along the length of Eleanor's. The warm, still firm flesh melded to her and she felt herself descending into sleep. Beautiful, she thought, that at least is not the truth, and then joined Eleanor in oblivion.

Mr Edmund Burke concurred with Sarah's doubts. A sophisticated and sensitive man, more literary than legalistic, he still wrote as a lawyer to the Ladies, telling them of his belief that the law would not censor the press on such a matter, as it surely well deserved. He wrote that he felt indignant at the clear injustice the article had done them. But he was careful to add that he thought it would be very difficult to get redress from the courts.

'Your consolation must be that you suffer only by the baseness of the age you live in, that you suffer from the violence of calumny for the virtues that entitle you to the esteem of all who know how to esteem honour, friendship, principle, and dignity of thinking.'

As they circled their Place one late morning during a cool August the Ladies read Mr Burke's letter. Sarah was secretly relieved that the matter was now at an end. Eleanor's cough had grown worse and Sarah was more concerned for her beloved's health than for the world's good opinion. As they walked, the catarrh in Eleanor's chest seemed to hamper her breathing. They walked at a slower pace to allow her to take short breaths. The cough had forced her voice into a deeper register than it usually occupied.

'So Mr Burke despairs of the law for us. It means that in his heart, beneath his professed sympathy and indignation, there resides the belief that we have *not* been maligned. Of course. That is what the letter means.'

Sarah did not reply. Eleanor coughed, bringing up into her mouth a ball of phlegm. She turned her head and rid herself of it into the garden border. Sarah felt faint. Before her eyes rose the picture of the soiled Woodstock fountain and then the stained corner of the sitting room and Sir William. . . . She swallowed with difficulty. Then she said: 'Oh my love, *not* in the laburnum bed.'

Of such small remonstrances are the silences made that batter at the walls of human relationships. Eleanor said nothing then or throughout their supper. She spent more time than was customary with her accounts and the day book, in which she was careful to note the receipt of Mr Burke's epistle. She followed that with a memorandum: 'Permit few visits and no stopovers.'

In bed that night they did not indulge in their customary talking out of 'sweet sorrows' but lay side by side separated by a significant inch of paillasse, by thoughts of Mr Burke's desertion, by Eleanor's defilement of Sarah's sacred weeding place, by ordinary occurrences that gradually work their way into all unions, like termites, sometimes making them vulnerable later, to larger, more damaging assaults. In every respect, theirs was a true marriage.

*   *   *

Sarah had found a staunch shield against her lifelong tendency to sadnesses, a new sphere for fantasy that occupied much of her reading and thoughts: Methodism. Her Protestant spirit had always been stronger than Eleanor's long abandoned Catholic principles. Sarah cherished her letters from churchy Julia Tighe. Her responses to them were filled with references to God, morality, faith and works, and Methodist theology. In turn, Mrs. Tighe ventured to wonder if it would be convenient for Mr John Wesley to call upon the Ladies.

Eleanor would have nothing to do with John Wesley. When Sarah opened her prayer book Eleanor moved to a chair at the other end of the room, as though aware of a noxious aura of religion surrounding all such objects and the words within them. To her, prayer was an admission of weakness, a denial of the camaraderie between them, a confession of cowardice, an acknowledgement of the failure of sacred human will. She saw Sarah's faith as an abdication of personal, private power to an unseen, mythical figure whose worth, whose very existence, she argued with poor Sarah. During Eleanor's secular diatribes Sarah remained silent. Her Christianity had few sectarian bounds: she searched at Valle Crucis for the pieces of the True Cross said to be embedded in one of its ruined walls and was hurt when Eleanor ridiculed her efforts.

Each Sunday, Eleanor accompanied Sarah as far as the door of the Church of St. Collen in the village. While Sarah worshipped, Eleanor walked the stark fields behind the village in all directions, returning in haste if she spied a bull in the next field—or even if there was the possibility of the presence of a bull—while Sarah prayed, offering her sins to the mercies of St. Collen, once Abbot of Glastonbury, a noble Briton who, in his youth, killed a pagan knight in defense of his faith.

Eleanor waited at the door of the church, wearing her royal blue velvet habit and silk top hat, her only acknowledgement of the day. For the occasion, Sarah wore a gown, a bonnet, and shawl, although she knew Eleanor considered this an unworthy concession to parochial custom, a defection from their agreed-upon costume.

Walking home together, Sarah attempted what she considered an appropriate topic for Sunday conversation: 'I learned today that St. Collen never recovered from his guilt at having killed a man, even though his victim was a pagan. He resigned his post as abbot because more than anything he desired to attain the full peace of a recluse.'

Eleanor celebrated the end of the weekly hour of their separation by being conciliatory. She was willing to listen.

'We both understand that desire. We have felt it ourselves. Except these days we seem to achieve it less and less.'

Sarah pressed on to complete her lesson in hagiology. She never gave up hope of finding a weak spot in Eleanor's defense against the God that seemed so real and present to her.

'He found a cave not far from here, the minister told us this morning, in a bank of the Dee. Now, no doubt, it is long since washed away and disappeared, carried off by the fast-flowing river.'

Eleanor wanted the holy legend to be finished before they arrived at Plas Newydd and the chicken boiled in broth that Mary-Caryll had promised for their dinner. 'And then?' she asked, suggesting some urgency.

'It is said he lived the rest of his life in that cave, many,

many years. It was there that he wrestled with the Devil, the Power of Darkness, the awesome Lord of the Unknown.'

'Did he win?'

'Who can know? Only God, I believe, keeps account of those mortal battles.'

'I suspect that, like most human battles, he may have been soundly defeated. Why else is the world so filled with misery and pain?'

'I don't know. But he is called a saint, which must signify that ultimately he won his private war against Satan.'

'Perhaps. Did Mary-Caryll mention what greens she was preparing for dinner?'

Sarah had grown used to Eleanor's abrupt change of subject when the discussion was related to God. It no longer angered her. She went valiantly on, trying to complete today's lesson to Eleanor: 'We live here, in a village named for St. Collen. Llangollen means the land that surrounds the church of St. Collen, I believe. So his struggles may well be destined to be repeated in the lives of everyone living on his ground. Even on our small portion of it.'

'Perhaps. But I don't believe it is so. . . . Well, then. It might be asparagus. Yes,' Eleanor said as she opened the gate and stepped back to allow Sarah passage ahead of her, 'I remember now. She *did* say asparagus in butter sauce.'

The odd thing about the delicate matter of belief that hung between the Ladies like a spider web, hardly tangible but still visible to them both, was Eleanor's own set of convictions. The older she grew—she was now in her late fifties—the more she trusted the efficacy of magic. For the amelioration of her terrible headaches she believed in elephant's hair laid upon her brow. Dried tiger's feet, she thought, placed over the placenta, removed stomach ache. From a dealer in Edinburgh she ordered samples of exotic teeth: walrus, whale and seal dents, which she kept in a camphorated box and removed on the occasions of tooth-ache. She had read that one or another of these, placed on the tongue, would communicate the great power of their beast to the sufferer's pain.

When Sarah turned to John Wesley's theology, Eleanor countered with a dedication to Gothic matters. For some time she gave serious thought to the need of a tunnel under the full length of the house. At first it was a romantic concept. The possession of an underground passage gripped her imagination.

'We can go from the library to the herb garden without once being seen.'

'Why should we wish to?' Sarah inquired.

Eleanor had no ready reply. She abandoned her plan to have Mr Lewis and Mr Jones collaborate on digging and construction. Later on, during the blood-letting on the continent, when aristocrats were suffering violent fates, and Eleanor feared revolutionaries in the British Isles would catch the fires of rebellion, she again raised the subject of an underground tunnel. This time Sarah's sympathy for the project was engaged. The two women often lay awake expecting the arrival of the French and Irish rabble at their door. An underground tunnel now appeared to be a ne-cessity, a place in which they might escape the democrats intent on rape, pillage, and arson.

But the idea of a passage, compelling as it was, fell before the estimate of its cost. Mr Jones said it was beyond his skills to accomplish, and Mr Lewis, who knew very well *he* could not make a tunnel, placed an impossible price, forty guineas, upon its accomplishment. Reluctantly Eleanor abandoned the plan.

More: Eleanor ordered from her booksellers in France, in Scotland, in England, every volume they had on witch-craft and sorcery, on ghosts and haunted places. Each week, from first page to last, she read the *Times*, searching for stories of the occult and the supernatural. From that paper she cut a story of one Mr Weed, who retired to the Tower of Ludworth Castle in order to rid himself of the evil in him. Here, Eleanor decided with evidence provided her by other books on the subject, he might have offered sacrifices to the Devil, flagellated himself, and then col-lected the blood from his torn skin, which, during the ritual he performed each evening, he drank mixed with vinegar. It was, she had read, the form of a Red Mass.

'If you are right, it is the Devil he is communicating with,' said Sarah.

'Perhaps so. But the newspaper says that after a few months in residence in the Tower he locked its door and threw the key from a window to the ground below.'

'And then?'

'When the door was opened by his servitors to rescue him, he was not there.'

'Not there? Gone, *all* of him?'

'Everything. No one has explained it. My suspicion is his body was taken away by spirits conjured up during his Mass.'

'Oh love, do you really believe that?'

'Does it seem impossible to you?'

'Yes.'

'My beloved, you have said you believe that Jesus was removed from his tomb by angels. Is that not more impossible?'

Or:

'I see here that a Sussex woman purports to lay eggs.'

'Oh what foolishness,' said Sarah.

'Is it more foolish, do you think, than to claim to have borne a child without a father?'

Sarah was aghast at the comparison: Our Lady who bore Our Lord and a mad vixen of a woman who claimed to be—a hen? She could not speak.

Once, Eleanor hired Mr Lewis to drive The Hand's chaise to Wrexham so that she and Sarah could watch a snake-charmer perform. Sarah went unwillingly, opposed to such exotic matters but bound to her friend by time and vow. Eleanor was delighted with the snake's absolute obedience to the summons of the flute, its straight, upright body rising slowly, at a command, out of a jug, its wise eye and flickering tongue under perfect control.

But the witchcraft and magic she so sought out finally came home to her, in Llangollen. Mrs Edmunds's small son Stanley had begun to fail. After Eleanor had visited him in his bed at The Hand, she came out to tell Sarah that he looked to be almost a skeleton. They stood together in front of the inn, debating what might afflict the poor child. Mrs Edmunds spied them from an upper window and rushed down to speak to them.

'We have seen your son,' said Eleanor, using the royal plural, the pronoun she employed for all her experiences, and Sarah's.

Mrs Edmunds shrieked: 'Shanette. It was Shanette.'

'Who is Shanette?'

'You must have seen her. She's ninety-nine, they say, the oldest person in the parish. The beggar woman.'

'I have seen her,' said Sarah, careful not to add that Eleanor had told Shanette never to enter their gate again after she had come to the kitchen door and, in revenge for the meager tea she had been offered, scratched a five-pointed star into the fine new wood.

'She begs for charity here every Sunday,' said Mrs Edmunds, still at the top of her voice. 'And feast days. She stands at the front and my lodgers are bothered. Six weeks past, I chased her off. As she went, little Stan ran across her path. She reached for him and caught him and turned him to her before I could be out to him. I saw her give him a long look, an evil look from those old yellow eyes she has. Next I know, poor Stan begins to wither away in his clothes there. Now he says nothing and hardly goes out. He droops and is so quiet and will not eat.'

'She must be a witch,' said Eleanor positively, delighted identification ringing in her voice. 'Tell the carpenter the tale. Mr Jones and I have discussed such matters. He'll know what to do.'

Edward Jones did. He took a pin from the child's pinafore. For nine days, mornings before sunrise and evenings after sunset, he came to The Hand, sought out little Stanley, held the pin over his head, and read a prayer of his own composition. Then he searched the village until he found the witch Shanette, who had made a shelter for herself under the far arch of the River Dee Bridge.

'Kiss this,' he commanded the old woman. She was delighted to obey, believing that he intended to inflict the pin upon some deserving victim. So she did as she was bid. Then the carpenter murmured 'God Bless it' nine times and returned it to the child's clothing. The next time he had occasion he knocked on the kitchen door of Plas Newydd.

'Little Stanley Edmunds is better,' he told Mary-Caryll. 'He is fatter now and always hungry. Please tell your mistress Lady Eleanor.' He gave Mary-Caryll all the details of his curing method.

The story was brought to Eleanor while she sat in the library bay window reading *La Nouvelle Héloise*. Sarah sat close to her, listening and netting a small purse for Mrs Tighe's birthday.

'Edward Jones has been, and says little Stanley Edmunds is recovered in health.' She repeated the sentence twice before Eleanor looked up from her book.

'So,' said Eleanor. The single syllable was full of pleased complaisance. 'Thank you for bringing the news.'

Mary-Caryll went back to her butter making.

Sarah said: 'It was the prayers.'

Eleanor smiled. 'Perhaps. But far more powerful is a witch's kiss. And the pin.'

The day book: 'My sweet love and I talked of Rousseau.' A few days later: 'From 12 to 3 I read Rousseau to my Beloved.'

La Nouvelle Héloise was translated into English after its huge success in France, where five editions were issued from 1761 until the Revolution. It came to the Ladies' library as a gift from Julia Tighe with the best of intentions: to provide Sarah, at least, with a model of true marital virtue. She could not have guessed that the Ladies would read the moral letters that composed the story in the light of their own lives. The tale of premarital love that turns into an example of marital virtue was seen by them as a rubric for their own situation, a reflection of the model society they believed they had created for themselves. In their minds, Rousseau had reinforced their illicit attachment to each other. They believed he was their author, their philosopher and guide, and that he may even have had *their* revolt against custom in mind when he created Julie d'Etange and Saint-Preur. Had they not discovered, like Rousseau, that virtue blossomed when persons dealt directly and simply with each other? Did not the young girl and her beloved tutor resemble the Ladies themselves when Julie, the redeemed sinner, lay dying because her tutor has been sent away? Was Saint-Preur not smuggled into her sickroom, where a superbly romantic and passionate reunion saved the dying girl? More than that, did the lovers not believe, indeed *know,* that they were not sinning because their love was both simple and natural, because in the eyes of God they were married? Were not their souls elevated beyond the common man's ground by the beauty of the world they had constructed around them, where every vista raised the spirits to heights of metaphysical pleasure, each moment of delighted contemplation fed on the beauties of nature? In this way the Ladies talked on and on to each other of the novel they both so loved, and of themselves.

La Nouvelle Héloise became their text, the homily for their days, their walks, their nights together. At first, the willingness of Julie to marry her father's friend Wolmer after years of passionate love for Saint-Preur, had disturbed them. But they came to recognize that Wolmer's was a great heart and mind, his the philosophy of the will directed to the higher good, trained to the acquisition of virtue.

'How extraordinary it is. He knows full well that Julie has loved Saint-Preur and yet he is large-spirited enough to invite him to live with them, and to tutor their children.'

'He believes he has remade Julie, stimulated her to

innate goodness. He has a great faith in her new person, has he not?'

Sarah wondered. How did Julie and Saint-Preur learn to control their passion for each other? By accepting Wolmer's theorising? By example?

She reread Julie's last letter before her death. She asked Eleanor: 'Does it not turn it all around, so that Wolmer's lessons . . . are not entirely successful? Even, questionable in their ultimate effect?'

But Eleanor was quite sure of the existence of human reform: 'She is dying, of course, a wonderful end because her death results from saving her drowning child. She has said in other letters that in every respect her life is a happy one. She asks Saint-Preur to marry Claire, her widowed cousin, who loves him.'

'Yes. But somehow, it seems, in her last moments, that her thoughts are with Saint-Preur rather than with her husband. All Wolmer has taught her has, somehow . . . fallen away.'

Eleanor could not abandon her position. 'We must understand the story in two ways. First, that true love, like Julie's for Saint-Preur, like Wolmer's for Julie and Claire's for Saint-Preur, like Héloïse's for Abelard . . . like ours, endures over all obstacles placed in its way by custom and rules. And then, that society's views of true love are stiflingly narrow, and always in terms of marriage. A union of the highest virtue, of two lovers whose minds and bodies come together simply and directly in beautiful places is not necessarily marriage. Marriage is a tired name, a legality, an announcement, little more.'

'What *will* we call what we have then?'

'Natural love, my dearest. In Rousseau's words.'

Sarah turned her head away so Eleanor would not see

the tears that rushed to her eyes. The splendour of their mutual desires, the sweetness of their companionship, the way the unimaginable had become 'natural': Sarah's throat closed at the thought. Her tears flowed freely down her cheeks.

They debated the implications of the novel as they walked their scrupulously raked stone paths, leaning together on each other's arms, like two elderly theologians engaged in exegesis upon a sacred text. Briefly they rested on a bench placed strategically to afford a view of the brook on one side, and beyond that, their huge potato garden on the other.

Mrs Tighe included in her letter to Sarah a detailed history of her neighbour, Mrs Long, who had been discovered by her husband to have been unfaithful with the minister of the local church. Sarah's indignation could not be contained. 'I think,' she wrote to Mrs Tighe, 'that a lady guilty of adultery should be branded with a great *A* on her forehead.'

Eleanor told Sarah to add: 'It is my opinion that such a woman should have her ring finger cut off.'

Always they said yes to the requests for temporary haven from aristocrats escaping the retributive injustices of the rebelling French peasantry. Madame de Genlis and Mlle d'Orleans stayed overnight at Plas Newydd, entertaining the Ladies at dinner with gruesome tales of trials by ruffians and imprisonment of their kin in the Bastille in the company of syphilitic prostitutes and street villains. Eleanor told the French ladies about the recent Dublin uprising that she thought might have been set off by the example of the revolution abroad. She was assured there was no comparison in brutality, viciousness, bloodshed, and terror.

Invited to stay on, Madame de Genlis refused. She had been driven to distraction, as she lay abed attempting to sleep on the first night, by the eerie moans of a harp, so successfully hidden from view that she could not find it to silence it. It twanged and sighed throughout the house the entire night. Next morning she packed her portmanteau and left for a village inn.

In her fortnightly letter to Mrs Tighe, Sarah wrote: 'It is Democratic and French Principles alone—which began with removing their God and their King—from whence such Diabolical Acts can proceed.'

Eleanor, the more conscious prose stylist of the Ladies, recorded her observations about rebellions in the two hemispheres: 'Fatally spreads the pestilential taint of insubordinate principles.'

When Anna Seward appeared at their door with no prior announcement of her intent to call, Eleanor sent Mary-Caryll to turn her away. So Miss Seward proceeded on to Lichfield, like Harriet Bowdler heartened by what she had glimpsed through the half-opened door: white-haired figures standing shoulder to shoulder peering from a side window. She was determined to return. By the next post she sent the Ladies a copy of *Louisa: a Poetical Novel*, her popular book now in its fourth edition. To the new edition had been added a frontispiece—a portrait of herself by George Romney. The tall, handsome, stern-faced woman the Ladies had glimpsed from the window had been metamorphosized by the romantic painter into a rosy, ringletted nubile young creature of sunny smiles and girlish countenance.

Dutifully, the Ladies read *Louisa* and determined that it was indeed poetical. They marvelled that a woman, writing under the guise of a man, could achieve so high-minded and extravagantly romantic a novel. Penitent, Eleanor sent a thank-you letter to Miss Seward, acknowledging the receipt of 'the beautiful story.' Miss Seward responded by mentioning she would be leaving Edinburgh after a spring visit and returning for her summer stop in Bath. A somewhat circuitous path might bring her to Llangollen.

'She must be wealthy,' observed Eleanor. 'All that traveling.' And then she added, not so much a *sequitur* as a sudden idea: 'Shall we invite her to visit?'

'To stay the night, do you think?' Sarah asked.

'All right. To stay the night.' It was the grand concession.

At three in the morning the three women were still in the landing sitting room, talking. For once Eleanor had not activated her aeolian harp, whose keening usually made visitors fearful that nocturnal spirits were howling for entry at the windows. A beneficent quiet in the house, the servants and animals long since bedded down, the dogs asleep at Sarah's feet, Anna Seward told the Ladies of her life.

She was born in the house in which she still resided, in Lichfield Close, a Tudor home of generous spaces and age-old gardens, a gift to her parents by the bishop at that time, her father's distant cousin. Until this year she had occupied the same nursery quarters that were hers, and her sister's, and foster-sister's, as children. Upon her father's death (her mother had gone to her 'eternal rest' five years earlier) she had moved into her parents' wing of the house, thus taking on 'the feeling,' as she expressed it, with a smile, 'of being my own mother and father.' In those elegant rooms she wrote her poetry and fiction, and read widely in books such as John Hawkesworth's *Almoran and Hamet* ('What a beautiful story, how sublime its moral!' she told the Ladies). Many of her poems, she said, trying to suppress her evident pride, had been published in English newspapers and periodicals. At Lichfield Close she was thought to be a genius and was called 'The Swan of Lichfield.'

'And what of your sisters?' asked Eleanor.

'My sister, also named Sarah, was my beloved. We shared everything and planned to spend our lives together, much as you have been fortunate enough to do.'

Eleanor interrupted the narrative to say: 'We have *made* our fortune.'

'But my heart was broken when my father announced she would marry a Mr Porter, a nondescript, pallid fellow who is the late Samuel Johnson's stepson. And poor Sarah *agreed*.'

'No doubt you forgave her afterwards,' said Sarah, for whom reconciliation was always the main ingredient of love.

'She did not require it of me. On the eve of her wedding, as we lay close together in bed talking of the changes marriage would bring to our affection, she was feverish and complained of a severe pain through her temples. As I was accustomed to doing, I offered her a massage. I waited for a reply, but her eyes reddened, as though the sockets had filled with blood. Blood came from her nose, her mouth. I called her name but she did not seem to hear me. She died in my arms in a few minutes. Dr Erasmus Darwin, who was called, said it was virulent typhus.

'For some months afterwards, Mr Porter called at Lichfield, hoping, I believe, to persuade me to take Sarah's place in his marital plans. Naturally I rejected him.'

The Ladies sat quietly, looking on compassionately as Anna Seward wiped her eyes.

'How long is it since she passed on?' Eleanor asked with unaccustomed softness.

Anna Seward's voice broke: 'Almost twenty-five years last month,' she said, and then she added: 'I have never been able to read anything by Samuel Johnson since that time without loathing. My memories of that terrible man are so strong that I have taken to regular correspondence with Mr James Boswell.'

'Who is James Boswell?' asked Sarah.

'A sycophantic friend of his, an odious man who has written a biography of his friend. I cannot think it will come to anything, not with Johnson as subject.'

The Ladies made no comment. Eleanor silently decided to send for the works of Samuel Johnson, with which, she thought to herself, I am woefully unacquainted.

After a silence during which she seemed to recover from her sad memories, Anna Seward went on: 'I had, too, a beloved foster-sister, Honora. But her life was tragically ruined.'

'She too died young?' inquired Sarah, preparing to assume the appropriate sorrowful attitude.

'In a sense. She married. One Richard Edgeworth, whose first wife had died in childbirth. After Sarah left me, Honora and I lived together harmoniously for many years. She married late, and her husband is elderly with a grown daughter, Maria, who remains at home and dabbles in literature.'

'I think I may once have read something by Maria Edgeworth,' said Sarah softly, afraid to add she had rather enjoyed it.

'Terrible, terrible drivel. Without ideals, without sensibility, without any sympathy for the great human virtues.'

'Did you still see your foster-sister?'

'Not at all. I disliked Mr Edgeworth too much. And she, a beautiful and most amiable woman, grew coarse and thickened at the bosom and the waist. An unbelievable transformation of person and spirit. And I had loved her so. Then she died quite young in Ireland, of a wasting disease.' Again Anna Seward's voice broke.

It was very late. Sarah had grown visibly tired. Eleanor was still intent on hearing the full story of this interesting woman whose life seemed to have some elements of their own.

'Are you now alone?' she asked.

'Yes. After my father went, I was able to live in Lichfield Close on the generous competence he provided for me: four hundred pounds a year,' she added smugly. The open announcement of the amount surprised the Ladies, as later in bed they confessed to each other, rehearsing the dramatic narrative of Anna Seward's lonely existence, even with a 'generous competence.' But in Anna Seward they recognised an ally, another woman like themselves, someone else who had turned against society's tight prescriptions. 'Now,' they said to one another and smiled at their discovery, 'there are three.'

Anna Seward wrote, when she completed her tour, from Lichfield: 'I am inspired by you and y^r elegant Place to write some verse. It is titled "Fairy Place in the Vale." '

She enclosed a many-stanza'd poem. Eleanor recorded the best quatrain in her day book:

> *'Happy is he who such shades retires*
> *Whom nature charms and whom the muse inspires;*
> *Whom humbler joys of heartfelt quiet please*
> *Successive study, exercise and ease.'*

Harriet Bowdler languished for invitations to Plas Newydd. She took to writing bulky, very long letters. She badly wanted Sarah's attention. Her letters were full of girlish, foolish expressions of affection. While the letters were addressed to both Ladies, Harriet's intention was clear: to engage Sarah's devotion. Sarah was careful to omit the first person pronoun from her responses, hoping by her example to teach Harriet the appropriate approach to their household. Slowly Harriet came to understand that it would not be wise to alienate Eleanor. She decided to write to each Lady separately. To Eleanor she affected what she regarded as a jocular tone, addressing the Lady with extravagant endearments as though she were a male suitor, calling Eleanor 'The Viellard.' The pretense that 'he' was in love with the elderly Eleanor and hoped to persuade her to marry 'him' sickened Eleanor. Through Sarah, she let it be known that she did not find Harriet Bowdler's fantasy amusing. Later, she regretted this move when she found that the avid Harriet, hungry, indeed starved for affection, directed all her need for love into a single vessel, Sarah.

> 'To luncheon: the Russian Ambassador,
> Count Woronsov'

'To Dinner: Peter La Touche & wife.
            Bishop of St. Asaph's daughter,
            Miss Shipley.'

'To Call in evening: William Owen, informed
                     Egyptologist.
                     Friend of Anna Seward, Mr Lester who
                     gave me names of bks on Pompeii.'

'Visited, Thrsdy-Frdy: Lady Bedingfield.'

Many called during the day but few remained the night
to sleep in the State Bedroom. In summer and in good
weather the Ladies were inundated with callers. They had
'only our small peace,' as Sarah wrote to Julia Tighe. She
herself often welcomed the flow of people. Eleanor, however, wondered if the very reason for the existence of Plas
Newydd was not being threatened, if their 'sweet seclusion' was not in itself a temptation to others to invade
it. Their 'retirement' was interrupted, the 'blessed peace'
too often broken.

Visitors came to inspect 'the wondrous plantings,' they
said. But their true motives were more often to see for
themselves the amazing Ladies of the Vale in their now-
famous snowy white hair styles, notorious hats and habits,
heavy, solid, growing old, with their canes and boots,
walking in tandem about their fields, or, if the callers were
among the fortunate ones, seated across from each other
at their double desk in postures so similar they could be
taken, at a distance, for symmetrical plantings or identi-
cally trimmed bushes.

Eleanor's migraines continued to plague her. So constant
were they, so often was she forced to retire her eyes from

use, that at first she did not notice the decline in her vision. Less and less was she able to read aloud to Sarah; Sarah took over that responsibility. When they walked, Sarah fell into the habit of leading rather than leaning upon her beloved friend. It was Sarah who noticed, on a cold November day, that a family had come to occupy their neighbour, the weaver's house, he having died at the age of ninety-two only a month before. Eleanor had not seen them arrive. She was unable to make out the five children playing in the overgrown garden, the brutish-looking woman hanging clothes on a cord between two trees ('within sight of our Shrubberies!'), the man with one eye gone and a long scar from the vacant socket to his chin.

'Strange that Mr Edwards would allow such people so close to us.' Eleanor sent Mary-Caryll to find what she could about them. Mary-Caryll, grown stiff and rheumatic after she had taken a bad fall over a cat, went on the errand, and returned with a report.

'Blanche Moses is the woman's name. The man is Lem.'

'Lem Moses?'

'I canna say. She said Lem, only that. The children are dirty and roughing about all the time. The oldest boy has no teeth in front. Two of the girls have spotted faces.'

That settled it. Next morning Mary-Caryll was dispatched to the landlord. His son John, a younger replica of his father in appearance and manner, came at once.

'My father ails, is not expected to live to Christmas, I fear. I came in his stead.'

Eleanor stared at him with her cloudy eyes. 'He is spry enough to provide us with disreputable neighbours,' she said. 'I want them put out.'

John Edwards hesitated. Then he said, in a low, apologetic voice: 'They are homeless ones. He lost an eye in the mines and canna find other work. He is to look for it here. We rented the house to them until . . . Well, my lady, the house is small for all of them. They won't be wanting it long.'

Eleanor rapped her crop against the back of the oak chair she stood beside. 'I want them gone, Mr Edwards, before week's end.'

John Edwards looked pleadingly at Sarah. Sarah put a hand on Eleanor's arm and started to speak.

'Out,' Eleanor said loudly and turned away. Sarah helped her to a chair near the New bay window. Eleanor sat down, staring ahead at what she took to be their chickens roosting on the roof of the coop.

John Edwards saw there could be no argument about the matter with the Lady. Without bidding the Ladies good-bye, he went back to the kitchen to speak to Mary-Caryll on his way out the kitchen door, the door to which everyone but royalty and distinguished persons came. He told her the Moses's story. Quickly he learned that Mary-Caryll had no sympathies independent of her mistresses. The stalwart Bruiser of old had grown crotchety under her physical infirmities and the years of heavy work. Now all she required was peace, to be left alone to rule her kitchen, the maids, and the kitchen gardener, and to work for Sarah Ponsonby when she could. In her own eyes Miss Mary had become one with the Ladies. Not for the world would she intervene in any matter about which they felt strongly.

Eleanor sat in the gazebo dressed in her heaviest jacket. Over it she wore her cloak. It was mid-March and still very cold. The gazebo had been recently constructed, on high ground behind the house, so the Ladies might be aware of the comings and departures of travellers and the approach of friends and strangers. Impatiently, she awaited Sarah's return from her evening survey of the vegetable gardens. Sometimes they did not make the Home Circuit together at the end of the day, for now Eleanor's strength was sufficient for only one walk a day.

When Sarah returned she was full of her discovery. 'Think of it, my love, this soon in spring. I have found a full-grown artichoke! Two months earlier than I can ever before recall.' She put the vegetable into Eleanor's hands, kissed her upon the lips, and sat down on the bench facing her.

'Lovely. We will share it for our lunch tomorrow. With fresh browned butter.'

Sarah said: 'It will be fine with a bit of lemon. The butter makes us heavy.'

Eleanor never took kindly to suggestions of change in their menus because of her weight. She had grown close to fifteen stone and breathed heavily when she walked. The stairs to their upper storey had become particularly onerous. For her, eating well and fully was a pleasure she would not agree to abandon. Sarah's concern for her health over the gratification of her palate made her angry. Her mouth set hard into its determined lines.

'Shall we walk a bit to the dairy to bid dear Margaret goodnight? I have the lantern here.' Sarah's question was a statement of intent, for the walk to the dairy was ritual. They had taken the short trip every night since Margaret had taken up residence in the dairy thirty-two years ago.

Slowly they went, Eleanor straining to see into the dark, Sarah holding her arm to steady her, to reassure her after the bit about butter, of her love. As they had grown older, the strong current of passion that had for so long sealed them together had settled into the connective tissue of companionate affection. They did not trust separation: never were they far from each other, either in the garden or in their house. Always they occupied the same rooms for recreation, ate meals in each other's company, entertained their visitors from their places on the same love-seat. In more than thirty years they had never slept a night out of each other's arms. The Oswestry compact had held.

As the evening deepened they came to the dairy and called out to dear Margaret, now fat, inert, and useless but, they believed, still quite able to recognize their approach. She had grown too old and too heavy to be able to stand. Her two calves, now almost elderly themselves, provided almost no milk. They lay together in the straw behind Margaret. The new heifer Julia, named for Mrs Tighe, who had raised Sarah's allowance in the past year, groaned softly as she heard the Ladies enter the dairy.

But they had come to see old, dear Margaret, a marvellous creature to the whole neighbourhood. At thirty-five, she was older than any cow the villagers could remember, an almost mythic figure kept alive, the Ladies thought, by the intense force of their affection for her. Sarah left Eleanor standing at the entrance, talking to the cow:

'Dearest Margaret, sleep well this night,' she said. Sarah returned with two handsful of barley, which Margaret loved. They listened to her munch with her hard, brown, toothless gums, like a very old person. Sarah massaged her ears, the white top of her head, and then reached down to scratch between her forelegs. They both repeated their goodnights in soft, endearing words. Sarah swung the lantern a little ahead of their footsteps to aid Eleanor's progress to the house.

The next afternoon they were seated under the trees. It was unexpectedly warm for March, so, at three, Mary-Caryll set the table out of doors and served their dinner, reminding Sarah, nostalgically, of dinners at Woodstock under the great elms. They had finished their dessert, strawberries and thick cream. Eleanor's starched shirt, clean in the morning, was now dotted with butter from the artichoke and sugar from the strawberries. Sarah was placing dishes on the tray for Mary-Caryll to bear away when she saw the Moses 'tribe' (as Eleanor called them) leaving the weaver's cot, led by the man who wielded a switch from one side to the other as he walked. The woman behind him bore baskets on each shoulder, the children came behind her, each carrying bulky bundles. Sarah described the procession to Eleanor, who smiled and made no comment. Trailing the group was the oldest boy who, like the man, carried nothing. He wore a low, saucer-shaped hat, the brim almost covering his eyes. Sarah could make out that part of the time he walked backwards. He seemed to be staring at them, or at their house, at least in their direction. When he turned towards them Sarah could see the round open black hole of his mouth. Then he turned away and followed the others.

At one in the morning an unidentifiable cacophony awakened them. Eleanor thought she had forgotten to take down the harp. But then they realized it was the cows. They heard the heavy sounds of Mary-Caryll walking about downstairs and then her excited voice, full of the old Irish accents:

'Something is on fire!'

Sarah helped Eleanor out of bed and covered her night dress with her cloak. In their bare feet they went downstairs.

'Where is it? What is it?' cried Eleanor, angered by her inability to see out into the black night.

The sounds of high, bellowing grief reached them. They knew then what it was, where it was: the dairy was on fire. Sarah, the spryest of the three, put on her boots and started to run. Mary-Caryll helped Eleanor with hers and then took her elbow to guide her over the gravel path. Now the sky to the west was lit with yellow flame and the cold night air filled with the smell of sour, mortal smoke and the sounds of high terrified moans.

'Margaret. Dear Margaret. Let us hurry, Mary.'

Sarah, running ahead, was almost knocked from the path by the new cow, Julia, rushing, blackened and crying, her head raised with terror. 'Wait. Wait,' Sarah called to her, but Julia raced on, out into the field before the house.

The three women stood as close to the dairy as they could, held back by the heat and the smoke. The crying had stopped; the air was thick with the heavy odor of burnt hide. Sarah sobbed as she looked into the remains of the doorway. Eleanor's clouded eyes filled with tears. Mary-Caryll had fallen on her knees, crossed herself, and was saying the rosary to herself. But Sarah did not join her in prayer: Eleanor's scorn of such weakness had eaten away at her faith. As the fire died away the Ladies still stood, staring into the black remains of the three cows.

'They are gone,' Sarah told Eleanor.

'Dear Margaret too?'

'Yes. She must not have been able to rise to her feet. She lies just where we last saw her when we visited this evening, her head resting on the barley we left for her.'

'Poor, dear Margaret,' said Eleanor.

'May her soul rest in place,' said Mary-Caryll, struggling to her feet. Sarah gestured to Mary-Caryll, her fingers on her lips as she shook her head. Mary-Caryll understood her intent. Neither of them would tell Eleanor that the fire had consumed Margaret. There was nothing left of her except ash and bones, and burned hide, shrivelled, black and curled away to one side, like a stored carpet. Her great brown eyeballs had survived the holocaust in the dairy and rolled together near the door, two large marbles, close together and staring ahead towards the grove of beeches beyond the dairy door.

The Ladies mourned Margaret's passing for months. The Vicar of St. Collen's, who came weekly to teach them Italian, was asked to remember her in his prayers from the altar. They neglected to tell him that 'Margaret Ponsonby' (Eleanor stopped short at appending *her* family name to the cow's given name) was not a close relative of Sarah's. The new cow, Julia, was returned to them by a neighbour and housed in a shed, temporarily, until the dairy could be rebuilt. But her fright was so great that she never again gave milk and had to be kept on, out of sentiment, as a pensioner rather than a producer. Mr Lewis raked up the site of the dairy, shovelling 'the remains' into a deep pit he had dug. Before he covered the hole with soil, he added to it a flat brown hat with a wide brim he had found in the bush beside the dairy's back door. It was now scorched and rendered useless to anyone, he decided, by the thick layer of soot that covered it.

John Edwards came to the back door to inform the Ladies of his father's death and, almost in the next sentence, to tell them he wished to raise their rent three pence a quarter, bringing the total paid him each year to £12, 5s. 9p.

Eleanor was horrified. 'He has seen all the improvements we have made. Do you think if we refuse he will terminate our lease?'

Sarah reassured her that his father had always been fair to them and she believed the son would be too. 'Let us pay it. Do not worry, my love.'

Edwards was a young man, and patient. He expected the acclaimed Place they had created would soon be his. Were they not old women, especially the Lady? He confirmed their lease at the higher rental and agreed it would not change in the following ten years. Then he settled back to wait.

Others came to call. As Eleanor's sight failed, she enjoyed conversation more and more. But she stubbornly maintained her criteria for admission: manners and title. Sometime after the turn of the century a gentleman dressed in comfortable country walking breeches caught up with them as they made their way across the Dee to picnic at Castell Dinas Bran.

'I am Mr Wordsworth of London, visiting with the Reverend Thomas Jones now retired from Oxfordshire to Llangollen. My wife and daughter are with him, walking ahead there. I am most honoured to encounter the famed Ladies of the Vale.' He offered his hand.

Eleanor did not notice it. She looked closely at him. 'Are you by any chance the poet William Wordsworth?'

'Madam, I am.'

Eleanor tipped her hat solemnly towards him. '*We* are honoured. We have read your poetry together, often, in the evenings. Will you and your family come to luncheon tomorrow?'

'Sadly, Lady Eleanor, we are travelling south early tomorrow morning.'

Eleanor hesitated. 'Well, then, today.' Rarely did she change an invitation to suit the convenience of a prospective caller. But a poet . . .

They all sat under the largest tree before the front door of Plas Newydd. To the tree was attached a painted board decorated with small daisies and violets. It read: *Ecco! Caro Albergo.* All around them, smaller trees bore other mottoes in Italian. Mr Wordsworth laughed a little with the Reverend Jones, who considered he too had been inivited, at the elaborate sentimentality of the sayings. The poet promised the Ladies he would compose a sonnet for them after he departed. Perhaps they would be able to find phrases in it to transfer to their signs.

Mr Jones was plump, his cheeks very ruddy, and he smiled constantly. Tufts of grey hair departed from his red skull at erratic angles. Eleanor was in a jovial mood and joked with Sarah about Mr Jones's healthy appearance, 'hardly suitable for one known as The Hermit of the Vale of Meditation.' For so he had been introduced to them by Mr Wordsworth. Gentlemen both, they refrained from pointing out that the same might be said of corpulent Eleanor living in well-advertised 'gentle poverty.'

From Ruthin, William Wordsworth mailed the sonnet he had written. It was titled "To the Lady E.B. and the Hon. Miss Ponsonby":

> A stream, *to mingle with your favourite*
> *Dee,*
> *Along the* Vale of Meditation *flows;*

So styled by those fierce Britons, pleased
   to see
In Nature's face the expression of repose;
Or haply there some pious hermit chose
To live and die, the peace of heaven his
   aim;
To whom the wild sequestered region owes
At this late day, its sanctifying name.
Glyn Cafaillgaroch, *in the Cambrian*
   tongue,
In ours, the Vale of Friendship, *let*
   this spot
Be named; where, faithful to a low-roofed
   Cot
On Deva's banks, ye have abode so long;
Sisters in love, a love allowed to climb,
Even on this earth, above the reach of
   Time!

Sarah thought it quite beautiful. Eleanor was furious when Sarah read it to her. 'To call our house "a low-roofed cot!" Insulting. Inaccurate!'

Sarah said: 'It was for the rhyme I believe, my dear one. The rest is very complimentary in the reference to my beloved Saint Collen, "the Vale of Friendship," "Sisters in love"—I think that is lovely.'

Eleanor muttered 'low-roofed cot,' and then said nothing else.

The poet returned to Llangollen a number of times but never again managed to gain entrance to Lady Eleanor Butler.

*   *   *

The Queen's potter had no difficulty gaining an audience. For his gift, Josiah Wedgewood brought an Egyptian-black fruit bowl with elegant white cameos embossed on the sides. He limped along after the Ladies to explore all the exotic beauties of Plas Newydd. He explained he had been lame since a boyhood affliction of small pox. His father had died soon after, and so his son became a potter at that age. As he departed, he pleased the Ladies by asking them to visit his factory in Etruria, an invitation he extended to very few, he told them. They collected such invitations from important persons: Eleanor listed them at the back of her day book with directions about how to reach places. Of course, they never went.

The gift pleased them more than anything. Eleanor had formed the habit of putting such presents on the long refectory table in the library. For each successive guest, the table was a stopping place on the tour of the house. Sarah, the guide since Eleanor had become uncertain of her footing, identified each one with the name of the donor, the occasion, the time of the visit. The Ladies had observed that the custom of displaying elaborate and expensive house presents generated more such offerings.

Their incomes had increased. Mrs Tighe died of tuberculosis, leaving a substantial sum to Sarah, and Eleanor's sister, killed in a carriage accident, increased her yearly gifts in her legacy. Their pensions were now paid regularly. At last they had become prosperous. Nonetheless, Eleanor's fear of poverty grew with affluence. Her judgments on her guests depended on the generosity of their gifts; she had increased her admittance criteria to three.

Some of the gifts: Lt. Colonel Arthur Wellesley, aide-de-camp to Lord Lieutenant of Ireland, brought magnificent book ends carved in bronze. Walter Scott ('a lovely man,' as Sarah described him in a letter, 'who writes novels') left a stuffed and mounted fox, killed during a hunt at his beloved Abbotford. It was distinguished by a handsome grey tail, erect and regal. Horace Walpole placed on their table a tooled-leather copy of his *The Castle of Otranto*, suitably inscribed to his hostesses. The sculptor Anne Damer donated a study for a head of her grandfather, Lord Milton, and a small drawing by Cruikshank, the master under whom she had studied art.

A letter comes from Anna Seward, now in her fifties, and, as usual, full of revealing autobiography: 'I have found a beloved friend. I resist the idea because I remember how terrible it was when Honora Sneyd married. I may have told you, perhaps not, but once she was wooed by Major John André, who died so bravely in the Colonies' War. How deeply was I a sufferer with Major André upon her marriage. We both lost her forever! My new attachment is a beautiful young woman who favours musk perfume, not unlike yours, my beloved Sarah. She is Elizabeth Cornwallis, whom I call Clarissa. Her parents are hard at work to persuade her to marry. But she refuses. Like my dear Vale friends, she despises society, loves reading, and favours the joys of solitude with me! Our friendship was inspired solely by my publications. Ours is a deep and loving friendship, although her parents forbid her my house. Our correspondence must be clandestine. I have not been too well this winter, the doctors are puzzled by my many symptoms and suggest it may be some form of scorbutic disorder. No doubt it will soon pass. I enclose with this letter a copy, made for me by Clarissa, of the fine review of my *Poems and Other Utterances in Fortnightly* and, so you may laugh, a vicious one by Horace Walpole, who says my poems contain "thoughts and phrases like my gowns, old remnants cut and turned." Did you know that effeminate fop is related to the glorious and talented Anne Damer, who is now travelling Europe with Mrs Piozzi? I send my ardent love to my most precious friends in their sweet and Blessed Vale.'

A letter comes from Harriet Bowdler, from Bath, addressed to Sarah as 'My Dearest Angel!' It concludes: 'O that I c^d shelter you in my arms and guard you from every danger. Fire. Wild villagers. Invaders into your privity. My peerless one, I feel for you even in your sacred Friendship. How terrible!' Sarah shudders and destroys the letter before Eleanor can see it and ask that it be read to her.

Servant problems plagued them. Early one September Eleanor persuaded Sarah to discharge the kitchen maid Betsy Haynes 'for Idleness, dirt and Such a Tongue!' The footman Edward Parry was sent away for making too free with the kitchen sherry. The gardener, Moses Jones, a source of irritation to Eleanor because he appeared to her to follow Sarah too closely as she directed him in his chores, was dismissed. In his place, Eleanor engaged a man-of-all-work, Simon, at a reduced wage, nine shillings the week. Now they had a worker who promised to do everything well, and failed to satisfy Eleanor in anything. Fourteen labourers now worked the farm, assisted with haymaking on the newly rented land, and tended the gardens. But these too were a transient source of help as Eleanor's temper flared at the sight of a man resting or stopping to take a drink of water from the well. She would send Mary-Caryll to threaten him with dismissal, and then discharge him if she saw him resting again. The growing staff was expensive. Eleanor records in the day book: 'Taxes on house, servants, dogs: £6, 6s. Income tax: £21, 6s. and 8p. Such an amount for the renegade Sir William Pitt to demand of two poor Ladies!'

Prince Puckler Muskaus leaves his carriage at the Lion and comes on foot to call. When Eleanor hears his trade has gone to the inn she so dislikes, for no reason that Sarah has ever understood, she cuts the call short, and turns the confused prince out after an abbreviated walk about the vegetable garden. Then, a few months later, Mrs Edmunds sends her coachman to present the yearly bill for the Ladies' use of her coach. Eleanor thinks it is excessive. She refuses to pay and sends the coachman away. Now the long relationship with Mrs Edmunds is over. Eleanor does not attend the funeral of her son Stanley, who has at last succumbed to a long series of mysterious illnesses. When the Ladies wish to travel abroad—very seldom now—they rent a chaise from a hostler at a new inn, The King's.

Eleanor believes all tradesmen are scoundrels and all professional men villains. During each contact with joiners, carpenters, chimney sweeps, thatchers, tailors, the strains grow great and then the relationship snaps. Eleanor damns them to hell and then sends them away. Sarah waits a diplomatic length of time and intercedes. Often they are re-employed.

*   *   *

Finally, they decide to resume their subscription to the *General Evening Post*, for their curiosity about the doings of the London world cannot be satisfied in correspondence. They read a story worth cutting from the paper, and they paste it into the day book in order to preserve it:

'It is reported that Anne Damer, the sculptress, second cousin to Horace Walpole, has been accused by Lord Derby of "liking her own sex in a criminal way." The object of Mrs Damer's "unnatural affection" is said to be the comedienne Miss Farren. Lord Derby, claimed by an acquaintance to be the protector of the beautiful Miss Farren, has forbidden her to meet Mrs Damer again.'

Harriet Bowdler sees the same article. She writes to Sarah: 'Few men know what real love is.'

Their days are filled with reading, walks, Sarah's knitting of stockings and gloves, and Eleanor's supervision of the bread baking and meat salting. Sarah does a great deal of sewing. She embroiders neckcloths and does gros and petit point for their chair seats. She stitches their initials on embroidered sheets and pillow cases. She re-binds their favourite books, tooling *EB* on the front leather cover, *SP* on the back. Eleanor oversees the milkings and churnings. She is the one courageous enough to wring the necks of turkeys when Mary-Caryll is ailing.

But there are moments when Eleanor's strength fails. A drunken man appears at the door, demanding food and money 'for a pot.' Eleanor in terror flees. Sarah comes to the door and speaks kindly to the inebriate. He takes the sixpence she offers him, tips his cap, and reels away.

Eleanor's fear of men has increased with her years. She imagines them hiding in the shrubbery, skulking about in their fields, in the doorways of the town. Sarah allows herself to show no outward sign of this phobia, but in her dreams . . .

'Wake up, my love. You are having a nightmare.'

Sarah sat up in their bed, staring wildly around the room.

'What were you dreaming?'

'I was *not* dreaming. I was there, on the Danish coast. A cold rain was falling. I was walking through a high, black forest on a path lined with black cedars. Suddenly it was no longer cedars but tall men in mourning suits walking in unison, stamping and coughing as they walked. I was between the two solid columns, unable to break through at either side, long lines of men-trees on either side of me. It happened.'

'All men, my love?'

Sarah was still engrossed in the reality of her vision. She lay back among the pillows and reached for Eleanor's hand.

'How do you know when something is real and when it is a memory? Or a fear?'

'I suppose you know when there is a transformation, when trees turn into men. That does not happen in the real world, on our walks, for instance, when cedars remain cedars.'

They lay close together. Eleanor held Sarah to her, stroking her hair.

'Can you sleep now, my love? Is it all over?'

'Yes. Most of it. The trees are gone.'
'And the men?'
'No.'

'Sarah finishes a White Satin Lettercase with the Cyphers in gold and a border of Shades of Blue and Gold, the quilting White Silk, the Whole lined and bound with Pale Blue,' Eleanor reports in the day book.

Two boys are caught on the Ladies' side of the Cuffleymen. Sarah accosts them, Eleanor grabs one and strikes him across the face with her walking stick. 'You have been stealing our strawberries,' she shouts. The one she beats is Mr Davis's son John, who runs home screaming to his father, his nose bloody, his eye closed from the blow. The other boy escapes. The Ladies go back to the house and report righteously to Mary-Caryll that they have caught the strawberry thieves.

Horrified, Mary-Caryll tells them *she* has picked the strawberries today as a surprise for their dinner.

Next day, Eleanor and Sarah walk to the village. At the Davis's door, Eleanor meets John's father. To Mr Davis she apologises. 'We were wrong in suspecting the boys of taking our strawberries,' she says. She asks to see the boy, whose face is still badly bruised when he comes to the door. Eleanor puts a shilling into his hand and says she is sorry. Then the ladies turn away for their walk back to Plas Newydd.

They accumulated goods, rented land, fertile and abundant flower gardens, streams and paths, and notoriety. After 1800, their plan for bushes, trees, and flowers executed to their satisfaction, they concentrated on the 'useful beauties' of vegetables and fruit. They raised animals for food and for sale at fairs, they bartered milk, butter, and cheese for services. They made money on their farm; Mary-Caryll added to her savings by selling her share of the produce to innkeepers in the village.

Their covenanted privacy had been invaded, not entirely without their complicity. In many ways these invasions were fortunate, for old age and worn custom had formed a crust over the passionate hunger of their earlier love, what Eleanor had once called 'the sweet union of our hearts.' They had learned the lessons that made living together possible: to bear each other's failings with fortitude and to freely indulge their own without guilt. They grew more and more like each other, their faults became common to them both, their virtues a kind of mutual feast that they celebrated together.

The longer they lived together, the stronger became their resentment of the outside world, a shared sentiment that bound them even closer. They believed the world continued to be silently critical of them; to them, expressed cordiality covered a malignant curiosity. Paradoxically, the more visitors they received, the larger their correspondence grew, the more gifts arrived to fill the tables in the library and overflow into the hall—the more their faith in the good will of humanity diminished.

Sarah's suspicion, her nagging worry, was that the fates were trying to punish them, to bring them down. Eleanor accepted prosperity, fame (or notoriety), gifts, in an Olympian spirit, believing everything was her due, tribute to the innovations they had devised, the acknowledged superiority of their united personages.

*   *   *

Each year in late April, on the anniversary of their successful escape, it was their custom to examine seriously the quality of their present lives and to renew their vows. Always the ceremony, if indeed their perambulations could be called that, took place out of doors, surrounded by the gracious botanical world they had created. Seated among the crocuses and anemones on the bank of the Cuffleymen, beside the grove of birches, or walking the paths they had so carefully laid out, they talked of the past and the present, they reviewed their accomplishments and holdings. On that day their steps took them to every corner of their beloved property, to the drying green, to the mushroom hut and the fowl yard, to the bosky aviary and the kitchen gardens, and beyond to the wide, full vegetable fields now beginning to show their dark green shoots, to the orchard where stood the new rustic shed with thatched roof.

Their gardens and their lives had followed the pattern set down by Henry Phillips in his book, which they had almost memorised. *Shrubbery Historically and Botanically Treated* taught them that 'Each walk should lead to some particular object. . . . The walker should be conducted in the most agreeable manner to each outlet and building of utility or pleasure.'

They made the complete Home Circuit, at each place of utility or pleasure stopping to remember the events of their past that had led so agreeably to the present: the meeting at Kilkenny Castle when Eleanor first looked upon the young face of Sarah Ponsonby and at once loved her, the day Sarah first spied the stalwart Eleanor Butler striding through the field at a distance and thought her to be the son of the house. They re-created the fateful first escape, the wondrous second one, the wandering year that in reality had been so terrible but now in memory was transformed into a series of pleasant, educational stops.

They promised each other to continue their studies in the next year: they would ask the vicar to teach them Latin. Sarah would work at greater accomplishment in her 'decorative arts,' their reading would expand into modern English writers, perhaps even Laurence Sterne. They would reduce the three hours an evening Eleanor gave to correspondence now that her vision had begun to trouble her. 'It must be saved, not wasted on others,' Sarah said. Eleanor agreed. They discussed their acquaintances (rarely did they think of them as friends with the exception of Mary-Caryll), those they would 'admit' again and those they had excommunicated forever, reviewing them as if they were soldiers on parade ground being inspected for endurance, continuing interest, and contributions to their household. Some few were labelled 'false and perfidious,' like those who, knowing no better, patronised The Hand, or others who were foolish enough to ask for the return of sums the Ladies had borrowed from them for some pressing purpose, like a meat or a bookseller's bill.

After the traditional walk and much talk, they always arrived at the moment of lustration in their lives: the wonder of finding and knowing each other, the still inexplicable miracle of their first love. They continued to be amazed at 'how we knew,' 'when we first thought,' how, from the limited possibilities their early existences had offered them, they had plucked their unique state of being that had coloured, shaped, and saved their lives, how they had realised a consummation granted to very few other women, they now were convinced.

In their own eyes they appeared as heroines of a great drama that had raised them above the 'common' level. They had triumphed over society's failures of imagination, their lives were rich and varied, their fortunes increased by legacies, and there were occasional but still extraordinary moments of bliss behind the curtains of their Bed. At such times, even now, they felt themselves among the Immortals, two persons chosen from birth, they believed, to walk a higher way. They seemed to each other to be divine survivors, well beyond the confines of social rules, inhabitants of an ideal society, of a utopia composed of strange and lovely elements of their own invention. They had uncovered a lost continent on which they could live, in harmony, quite alone and together.

As late as 1825, and only in her memoirs, did Madame de Genlis put to paper her opinion, for posterity, of the Ladies: 'Although to begin I found their way of life most impressive, even idyllic, I have come to think theirs is a wholly *mistaken* existence. I pity them greatly. Just as they will often drown out the comforting and *natural* sounds of night time with their odious harp, so they eliminate *natural* affections for other persons by their exclusive devotion to each other. Without children, without family ties, they are both victims of *l'exalte plus dangereuse de la tête et sensibilité!* How very sad! They are *chained* to each other forever!'

Before her death from gangrene, in 1807, Anna Seward had a serious falling out with Eleanor over a small matter of unreturned borrowed money. In her final letter, sent

from Ghent before she succumbed to the scurvy she had
been battling for some years, she told Sarah that she had
come to dislike Eleanor's 'harsh masculinity,' her violent
and arrogant nature. She had begun to wonder why Sarah
always acquiesced to her demands and to her terrible
temper. 'I do not pay her sufficient homage, I suppose,'
wrote Anna, 'and I make mistakes which offend her code
of behaviour. I cannot seem to please her and I no longer
have the wish or the strength to try. But you, my dearest
Sarah, you have lighted every day of my last years with
your sunny temperament. I will always cherish the sight of
your Fairy Place in the Vale. While I am in France attempting a recovery I shall miss you.'

Anna Seward, consoled against her disease by copious
potions of opium and brandy, died in a state of painless
exultation. She was brought back to Lichfield and buried
in the churchyard. Eleanor would not travel, so neither of
the Ladies attended. Reports in the newspaper, which they
read with interest and then cut and pasted into the day
book, listed a Miss Ellen Corkerly among the mourners.
She was reported to be the heiress to Miss Seward's entire
estate.

Anna Seward left Sarah a mourning ring.

Word came to the Ladies that plans were being formulated
to build a large cotton mill in the Dee Valley, only a mile
or so from Plas Newydd. The news brought Eleanor to bed
with severe migraine. Sarah sat with her, a day and two
nights, ministering to her sickness. As the pain receded
Eleanor was able to dictate a firm, commanding letter to
Mr Thomas Jones, owner of the land on which the mill
would stand, attacking the plans of the prospective mill

proprietors. The very idea of a mill was destructive to the peace of their valley, she wrote. 'Our quiet mansion's prospects would be destroyed, our precious retirement offended.' The health of all who lived adjacent to it was threatened. A new population of mill workers would be a danger to the morals of the village of Llangollen. Further, she wrote, 'enough merioneth is already being manufactured in nearby towns, and small cloth in Ruthin to satisfy the needs of trade.' She urged Mr Jones to give careful thought to the matter of taxes and rates, which would rise to an insupportable degree. 'Already, as you yourself must realise, they are sufficiently oppressive.'

Word of the letter, signed by both Ladies, reached the local newspaper, which reported, dramatically, that 'the fair recluses of Llangollen are leaving the Valley because of the cotton mill to be put up close to their cherished abode.'

The invasion was prevented. Not so the projected construction of the New Road. It was Thomas Telford's plan to build a great highway fronm Holyhead on Holy Island over the high-walled Stanley Embankment and through Angelsey, across a suspension bridge over the Menai Strait to Bangor, thence south east to Corwen and Llangollen, south from there to Oswestry, to Shrewsbury, to Birmingham, and ultimately to London. Racing for time against the plans of a Mr Macadam for a similar enterprise, Mr Telford, a shepherd's son, began his Great Irish Road, as some called it, the Telford Way in others' words, the Holyhead Road as it finally came to be named.

It was the anticipated passage of the Holyhead Road through their village to which the Ladies objected. The new turnpike would, they wrote in their long letter to the *Times* of London, 'crowd their streets and make noisy progress across the historic bridge over the Dee, still considered one of the seven wonders of Cymru. Our valley w^d be overrun with London—Dublin travellers who will not stop here to view the beauties that are here but will race through on fast and clattersome horses and chaises.'

The Holyhead Road, carrying Royal Mail coaches, became a reality, moving closer each year to Llangollen. The new weaver, Mr Cuddy, Mr Parkes of The Lion's, and other tradespeople to whom the Ladies were often in debt, came in a group to explain to Lady Eleanor and Miss Sarah the advantages of the road. A number of friends, among them Arthur Wellesley, Sir Walter Scott, Mrs Paulet, a painter in London, and the English actor Charles Matthews, wrote to tell them how much they looked forward to travelling to them when the new road reached their vale.

For the first time in recent history, Eleanor changed her mind. To the Telford Road Construction Fund, established in each county that might be benefitted by the road, she sent a contribution of one pound.

Mary-Caryll took sick during the haying season. Sarah sent one of the field men to the village for a messenger to be sent to the doctor in Wrexham. It was almost a week before one was able to come. By then it was too late. In the last months of her life Mary-Caryll was unable to walk, for she was afflicted with a crippling rheumatism. The big stalwart Molly was reduced to a joint-locked cripple. She remained in bed, on Eleanor's theory that rest might ease her frozen joints. When the doctor arrived, her lungs had filled with liquid. Sarah stood at the door to her small room watching her struggle against drowning. When the doctor lowered her wrist to the bed and covered her face with a sheet, Sarah sobbed loudly. She touched the still warm hand with its swollen knotty places as though to comfort her during her journey away from them. Then she went to tell Eleanor, who sat in the sunny New window, mumbling angrily about 'the idle, drunken gardener, Richard,' whose absence from the little piece of garden she was able to see could only be explained, to her mind, in most denigratory terms.

'Oh my love, she has left us. Our dearest friend is gone.'

They sat together, comforting each other in their loss. Eleanor's eyes, full of hot and painful tears, were fixed on the empty kitchen. Sarah cried copiously, her head on Eleanor's shoulder. Miss Mary's passing was mourned by the whole village. The Vicar of St. Collen's agreed to hold the service for her funeral in his church, although he could not offer her the proper rites of her Church.

Sarah and Eleanor followed the coffin, carried by The Lion's wagon and driven by Mr Parkes, to the church. Then they stood at the graveside within the close of the church while the body of their friend was lowered into the grave by four of the farm help. The square plot of ground in which she lay had been purchased by the Ladies. Some day they would there be with her.

The young Duke of Gloucester, the King's nephew, was waiting on their doorstep when they arrived home from the funeral. Always before, he had been granted admission at any time of the day or night that he happened to be stopping in the neighbourhood or passing through to London. This time, they told him, they had no heart for company and turned him away. The duke expressed his sympathy and said he understood entirely and would call again.

Inside the house, sounds of movement in the kitchen startled the Ladies. Sarah went to the back and found two acquaintances from the village, the two Hughes sisters, Anna and Helen, preparing their dinner.

'How good of you,' said Sarah. 'We had not thought of dinner, but how kind of you to think of it.'

The sisters smiled and went on with their cooking. Despite their grief the Ladies were able to eat heartily of the well-prepared dinner. With no prospects of their own, the Hughes sisters stayed on to take over Mary-Caryll's duties.

A month later, a bank officer from Aberystwyth called on the Ladies and presented them with an envelope. It contained bank notes, with heads of cattle printed upon them, in the amount of five thousand pounds: Mary-Caryll's life savings. She had left everything she had so arduously saved to 'my beloved Ladies, to make them both as safe as they have made me.'

Saddened, astonished by the generous spirit from the grave of their friend, they believed they knew Mary-Caryll's wish, without her having had to specify it. They sent Anna Hughes to fetch one of the Edwards. John came, looking very seedy and tired. His wife Jane ailed and was due to go to Bath for the 'treatment of the waters,' he said.

Eleanor had no time for amenities or sympathy. Her eagerness was barely disguised. 'Will you sell Plas Newydd to us?' she asked, in a tone more commanding than interrogating.

After many patient years, John Edwards was now ready to admit that the Ladies had outlived his expectations.

Besides, there was the money to be raised for his wife's cure and travel expenses. . . .

'I will, m'lady.'

'What price, Mr Edwards, will you demand of us?'

Mr Edwards thought of the largest sum he could imagine, thinking of the cottage near him that had recently been sold for a thousand pounds and some.

'Three thousand pounds, m'lady. Not a shilling less.'

1819. So. After almost forty years, Plas Newydd was theirs. They wept when the paper was brought to them, cried in each other's arms for the achievement of their dream to be secure and independent in their own Place. They wept for Miss Mary who had made it possible, and for themselves: who would be next to go, and how would the other survive the decimation?

When Walter Scott visited in the early twenties, he found the Ladies much changed. Eleanor was very heavy and almost blind. Sarah had grown dropsical. To her waist she was gaunt, her neck full of strings, her arms thin as broomsticks. But below her waist a great swelling had grown, so wide, so thick, that her skirts had to be gusseted in each side by one of the Miss Hughes. Her legs were not subject to the swelling that afflicted her abdomen. But their greatest pleasure, walking, was now difficult for them. Sarah's balance was affected; Eleanor's eyesight was uncertain. Always now, Eleanor walked leaning upon a cane, which she moved a little above the ground now and then to be able to detect obstacles. Still, arduous as it was for them, they were to be seen by visitors and villagers moving slowly over the Pengwern foothills or picking their way carefully along the outskirts of their demesne, or seated on the bench that girdled the great trunk of an elm, resting in preparation for walking again.

By 1821 Eleanor's writing in her day book had become almost illegible. Doctor Lewes in Wrexham examined her eyes, and told her the cataract formed over the left eye should be cut.

'Shall we have it done, my love?' she asked Sarah, as though the operation involved a mutual eye. Sarah thought if there were a chance that sight might be restored, it should be.

Eleanor told Dr Lewes she would submit to his knife. The day came, a bright, sunny, warm, late-spring day. Mr Parkes came for them and they set out in his chaise, dressed as they continued to be, even when their figures no longer suited the costume, in their riding habits, their cropped hair, still powdered despite their own white color, pushing out from beneath their well-worn, brushed beaver hats. During the long drive, Sarah held Eleanor's hand tightly and prayed to herself. 'Let nothing bad happen to my beloved, please, God.' With her suppressed prayer, she formed a deep resolution: to do everything she could to survive Eleanor. Without her, she knew, Eleanor would be unbearably unhappy.

The cataract cutting was brutal. Sarah sat outside waiting, covering her ears against the screams of pain. When it was over she led the shaking, bandaged Eleanor to the chaise and held her head to keep the eye from being jarred as they drove the miles to home. Eleanor went directly to bed and stayed supine for a week. Much of the time, Sarah stayed with her in bed, reading aloud and talking to her, easing her pain with cold cloths, whispering to her of the promise of full sight.

When Eleanor could be up and walking the paths again, or sitting in the library window to feel the sun on her face, she refused to wear the blue eye shield recommended by Doctor Lewes. Instead she dressed as usual, pulling the short brim of her beaver hat down over her forehead to keep the light from her left eye. Outdoors she surrendered and covered her cut eye with a bandage against the bruising noon light.

Two months after the operation the Ladies were compelled to make another trip to the surgeon, this time to question why the other eye had become strangely inflamed and painful. His examination confirmed Sarah's fears. Her prayers had failed. Much sight in the cut eye was gone and, because of Eleanor's age and the inflammation, there was little chance of saving the other.

Leeches might be effective, the doctor thought, or if not, a second cutting. Returned to home, and Eleanor back in their bed, Sarah applied leeches to Eleanor's temple, wiping away the blood that escaped the thirsty sucking of the insects. But under the treatment, the pain increased until Eleanor asked to be driven back to Wrexham. The second operation was worse—longer and more painful—than the first. Her convalescence extended into spring, preventing, for the first time in forty years, the celebration of their anniversary walk. But when she recovered and tried to walk the Home Circuit, when the perennial gardens began to flower and the grass was high enough to scythe and the orchard trees beginning to bud, it was found that Eleanor was totally blind.

*   *   *

William Wordsworth stopped to visit. Sarah was afraid to agitate Eleanor by the knowledge of his presence. Sarah and the poet walked to the farm building and the New bird cote, which he asked especially to see, while Eleanor sat in the library. Sarah permitted him to leave with nothing more than the brave sight of her beloved, glimpsed through the bay window, seated and comfortable, lifting her sightless face towards the sun. On the left side of her jacket Wordsworth was able to see that she wore her Croix de St. Louis, now a part of her daily dress, Sarah told him, sent to her by the French king in recognition of her ardent support of the Bourbon regime. Beside it she wore a large, gleaming fleur-de-lis, a present from Madame de Genlis before that lady had sat down to write her *Memoirs*.

Sarah's extended abdomen was disguised by her skirt, Eleanor's blind eyes had sunk into their sockets. The poet reported in a letter to John Lockhart: 'Lady Eleanor is surprisingly preserved for her eighty-five years and Miss Ponsonby at sixty-nine is in unimpaired health.' As they had always found it possible to do before, they had once again successfully disguised their true state of being from the world.

Sarah does no more bookbinding, for her time is occupied with the comfort and care of her beloved friend. Now a Mr Price in Oswestry is entrusted with such work. For Eleanor's eighty-sixth birthday Sarah has *La Nouvelle Héloise* rebound in an elaborate maroon velvet cover, with their initials combined and tooled into a single gold-leaf monogram on the front and back. Eleanor likes to hold it in her lap as she feels the fine covers, her thoughts often still on the intricacies and ambiguities of Rousseau's message.

Arthur Wellesley is welcomed by them both at the door. Eleanor takes care to address him by his new title, the Duke of Wellington. At dinner, she urges him to tell them his story of the last days of the war.

'Fifteen thousand of my good men died there. When the surgeon's report was brought to me at Waterloo I was sadder than I have ever been in my life before.'

Later, he sits on the low flowering bank, deep in violets and ivy, while the Ladies sit near him on a bench made in the shape of a ship's locker. Eleanor fingers her decorations as she listens, and Sarah cries softly. Tears run down the handsome, rugged face of the Duke of Wellington.

Softened by their sympathy he goes on to tell them, in his curious, mumbling speech, about his childhood, about his mother's view of him: 'I was thought too ugly for the priesthood or politics and therefore fit food only for powder. I outlived the powder, strangely enough, and proceeded to advance rapidly through the ranks of the military. Early, I had proposed to myself that I would get into Fortune's way, despite my mother's poor opinion of me. You will recall that I foresaw that the Bonaparte system was doomed. I'm most grateful that I survived my mother's prediction and lived to bring about its fall.'

'As are we,' murmured Eleanor, ignoring the clear evidence of the duke's high self-esteem. The duke was touched. From London he sent the Ladies two finely carved heraldic lions, which they placed at the entrance to their house, two great, noble beasts, tamed, couchant, protecting the gravelled path that led into a formal garden. Eleanor loved the beasts because they reminded her of solitary childhood games at Kilkenny Castle. Often as she passed beside the new lions, she reached to stroke one between its ears, smiling to herself. Sarah never asked the source of her smile and Eleanor never explained. It was her secret not subject to their half-century habit of total communication with each other.

When the New Place was theirs, they redid the downstairs rooms, lining the walls with carved oak, a decorative addition they believed enriched and strengthened them. The same heavy brown carvings were added to the hall and to the staircase. So pleased were they with the dim and romantic effect that they had workmen add dark wood panels to the porch. They ordered oaken canopies mounted outside over all the windows on the lower floor.

Sarah wrote in the day book: 'Rec'd from George Gordon Lord Byron a complimentary copy of *The Corsair* inscribed most agreeably to us.'

Sir Walter Scott writes to John Lockhart of his visit: 'I met them yet once again in their fowl yard, having only a few minutes in which to pay my respects. They were wearing heavy shoes and their usual men's hats. Now they seem to totter about, their petticoats tucked up to avoid the chicken messes. At first glance they might have been taken to be a couple of crazy old sailors, but when closer to them you forget the curiosities they are and see only their kindnesses, and their great and endearing devotion to each other.'

*   *   *

Forty-year-old Mrs Aphra Paulet had been recently widowed. She was childless and filled her empty days by painting romantic landscapes and pretty portraits of ladies holding their cherubic children. But she had grown tired of her lonely life. In the early days she had visited Plas Newydd a few times when Eleanor was still sighted and active and Sarah intent on carrying out her grand plans for the gardens. Mrs Paulet remained in correspondence with the Ladies, who, in the widow's fond memory, had never aged or grown fat or become ill. To her mind theirs was the perfect existence. After a year without Mr Paulet she wrote to them:

'I would very much like to make a third in your ideal ménage.'

She went into great detail, listing her assets, both personal and financial, and expressing her willingness to sell the property left to her by her late husband in order to join them on an equal footing. She reminded them that her artistic talent would be of assistance to them:

'I w^d immortalize in water colours the wondrous surroundings you have created and transfer your distinguished visages onto canvas with oil. These are arts in which many have said I have no little ability.'

Eleanor dictated a testy note to Mrs Paulet. And then, on second thought, she tore up the letter and never corresponded with the lady again.

General Isaiah York, a boy when the Ladies first came to Llangollen, remembered in years to come that Lady Eleanor's jacket fronts were always stained by melted butter dropped from the crumpets he had been occasionally invited to share with her after he had run some errand or other, and that her decorations were showered with hair powder.

Queen Charlotte sent a messenger over the New Holyhead Road to inquire if the Honorable Sarah Ponsonby could be persuaded to supply her with the plans of her 'miniature estate,' as she termed Plas Newydd. Sarah replied at once that she would be delighted to do so, but unfortunately, there *were* no complete plans, only sketches made over the years as the occasion required. These of course she would be honoured to send to Her Majesty.

To Madame Louise, a French Carmelite (and aunt of the French monarch) Sarah sent a hand-embroidered satin portfolio. The gift was in response to an eloquent and most flattering letter from the royal nun defending the Ladies' life of retirement against its critics, and assuring them that it bore a resemblance to her seclusion. 'It matters not at all,' she wrote, 'whether such a life be led under religious or personal auspices.'

An English novelist and economist, Miss Harriet Martineau, paid them a visit. In her diary, later published, she recorded her impression of two 'ancient dames with rolled and powdered hair and the stately manners of the past century.'

*   *   *

By the time Walter Scott recommended the novels of Jane Austen to their attention, Eleanor could not see to read them and Sarah was too impatient with the lady novelist's subject matter to become interested in the stories. 'They are all about marriage, and mothers and daughters,' she told Eleanor. 'Neither subject is of especial interest to us.'

In the last years their wine bill was high because Eleanor hid her resentment against her bodily weakness in sips of wine and liqueurs throughout the day and evening. They continued to purchase many books, far more than they would ever read. Their plans became chaotic, their expenditures foolish. They ordered sheets of marble and strips of carved oak intended for further wall decoration of their house but never found the right place for any of it. They did many favours for friends: wrote letters of introduction, helped them to obtain curacies and pensions. After such services were rendered, Eleanor sat back to await the opportunity to request a return, in services or in gifts, for their kindnesses.

Eleanor wrote for the last time in her day book on the evening before she went to Wrexham for the cataract cutting. She noted that it had been 'a Silent, Pensive day.' She said she was touched by 'my sweet love's affecting exclamations about my approaching trials.' She composed an epigraph:

> *Society is all but rude*
> *To this delicious solitude.*

* * *

1828: a cold and often fog-ridden winter. From January until March it snowed occasionally and then froze. There could be no walking about; the Ladies were imprisoned in their Place. The vicar sent to say he would not be able to continue the Latin lessons as his knee had swelled from a fall on their path following his last visit. No visitors braved the bad roads. Eleanor grew quiet, even submissive, allowing Sarah to lead her through their rooms, to decide what their sedentary occupations would be, to choose their reading matter. Sometimes she nodded while Sarah read, at other times her mind strayed to worry about the security of her possessions.

'Do you remember, my love, who borrowed our copy of *Vathek*? Has it been returned?'

Dutifully, and to put her mind to rest, Sarah went in search of the William Beckford volume but was forced to report she could not find it. Eleanor was agitated. Sarah promised to continue to look on the following day, and Eleanor seemed content. She sat quietly, touching the Cross of St. Louis on her jacket, a book in her lap.

Sarah went on with her reading although she felt Eleanor no longer listened. In the midst of *Michael* (left as a gift by an admirer of Mr Wordsworth's poetry) Eleanor asked: 'Are the doors well bolted?' and then: 'Do we expect dinner guests?' Sarah reassured her of their safety and their seclusion.

Now they received no one. It was Sarah's decision to save what time they had for themselves and to spare Eleanor the indignity of witnesses to her infirmities. Only once, and unknown to them both, was their complete seclusion broken. The new owner of The Hand, Mrs Parker (the Edmunds had sold the inn and gone to live near Snowden) had a daughter May, a young woman ambitious to become a painter of portraits. Three times she had requested permission to 'do' the Ladies' portraits. Sarah consulted Eleanor, who refused; she had always hated the thought of being 'pictured.' Now she was more adamant than ever.

The sisters Hughes, friends of May Parker, did a strange thing to the Ladies, whom they had served so faithfully for so long. They smuggled the painter into the house and stationed her behind the drawn curtains of the library window. There she sat, drawing the heads and upper bodies of the Ladies as they sat at their desk, one's hand resting upon the other's.

So, rendered by the brush of an untrained artist, posterity sees them: surrounded by books and all manner of small objects, their shoulders rounded as though they were each sheltering a secret inner core from common view. Sarah looks hard at Eleanor and Eleanor's eyes are fixed ahead on vast, dark space.

Eleanor died in her sleep, making no sign to Sarah, who slept undisturbed beside her. It was the twelfth of June, 1829.

All the shops in Llangollen closed on the day of the funeral. Many of the villagers put on black clothes. The wagon that bore the coffin from Plas Newydd to the church was draped in black velvet and drawn by a pair of fine black horses. Lady Eleanor's grandnephew, the Marquess of Ormonde and his wife, his five children, and Mrs Tighe's daughter, Lady Carolyn Hamilton, were among the mourners. To the villagers who lined the streets to watch the procession pass, it seemed a royal occasion. A large bouquet of flowers from the Ladies' garden, picked that morning by the Hughes sisters, lay upon the velvet covering to which was pinned the Ormonde crest.

Sarah sat in the library while the body of her beloved friend was taken away. She was so overcome that the sisters Hughes, standing to each side of her, were unsure how to assist her.

What she said to them was: 'I wish to be helped to our bed.'

Sarah did not attend the funeral, and so failed to witness the odd incident at graveside. A stray dog, whom no one present could identify and certainly, in its underfed and dishevelled state, no one wished to claim, stood among the mourners during the graveside ceremonies, and then followed them back to Plas Newydd. Next morning, Anna Hughes found him lying between the lions at the front door and led him around to the kitchen, where she fed him scraps. When Sarah resumed her short walks about the Place, he accompanied her. She named him Chance and treated him with respect because she had been told the story of his mysterious presence at St. Collen's and decided he was the last one to see her beloved.

For a new inhabitant of the Place, Chance rapidly became fiercely protective. Young Lewis Parker, about to leave for his school in September, came to ask Sarah if he might borrow a Latin dictionary. Sarah presented him with hers as a gift, keeping Eleanor's for herself. But Chance would not permit it. He beleaguered the boy when he tried to leave, howled at his heels, and would not be quieted until the boy handed the book back to Sarah. Then Chance went to lie in his chosen spot on the doorstep. When school began Sarah sent the *Dictionary* to the village in Anna Hughes' market basket, where it was dispatched in the mail coach to Lewis Parker.

The Duke of Wellington, who was not able to be present for the funeral, wrote to inform Sarah that he had obtained for her an additional pension of £200 to compensate for the revenue lost to her upon Eleanor's death.

For the first time, Sarah felt no pleasure at the thought of additional income. She was, she wrote to Julia Tighe's daughter, 'waiting to be allowed to leave.' She made her will, providing £24 a year for the Hughes sisters, and assigned the rest of her estate to the grandchildren of Lady Betty and Sir William Fownes. She bought no more books. Seated alone at their desk in the evenings, she reread the ones Eleanor had once read to her, hearing the beloved voice as her eyes passed over the words. She continued to be concerned about the well-being of their farm and the animals. She saw that the gardens were planted and weeded and that flowers were always in the house, the shrubberies shaped, the grass scythed. She oversaw the house cleaning, requiring of all the maids 'perfect neatness,' as she said. She was especially strict about the paths, insisting that the gravel be raked daily in careful, straight lines because, she said to the gardener, otherwise Eleanor might stumble.

During the thirty months between Eleanor's death and her own, Sarah was lonely but never alone. Her walks were companionable as she made her slow way, leaning on Eleanor's silver-headed cane as though it were her arm, to all the places they had loved to see, looking down the vistas they had cherished. She relished her morning turns over the Dee Bridge and often paused to look down. No longer did she fear the rushing waters through the central arch. She hoped that her long dream of submersion would somehow become a reality, as real as she had thought it to be during their first strolls in Llangollen. And when she returned, walking with her beloved friend down the long line of cedars they had planted, the trees stood erect, not once bending in towards her, never again assailing her with threatening corporeal shapes. She talked to Eleanor, who was there beside her. She pointed out to her the glories of the bank of the Cuffleymen, she told her it would not be long before they would have fresh artichoke again and then they would share it, with melted butter.

When she scolded the maids, her voice took on Eleanor's imperious tones.

She reassured Eleanor that she no longer needed to worry about the bell attached to her dead toe, for no longer did she fear being buried alive. She now wished so much for death that she did not need to be protected from any way that it might come to her. Many evenings she hung the aeolian harp in the window hidden by curtains. As she lay in their bed she listened with Eleanor's ears to its throbbing tones.

After a lifetime of crying at her fears and her life's small tragedies, she never shed a tear again.

Mornings before she arose, she listened for cuckoo and linnet and lark cries. When she identified them she asked Eleanor if she too did not hear the calls. She heard Eleanor's replies, always knowing exactly what she said. When they sat together having their dinner (for Eleanor's place was set, her chair drawn up to the table beside her own) Sarah watched for spilled food on her shirt front. With her own good eyes she saw the dear, blind face of her beloved. And because Eleanor had so hated it, she abandoned her Wesleyan dogma for a New faith, an ancient belief in the presence of her beloved.

Sarah went on sharing her life with Lady Eleanor Butler for two years, until the dropsy, as the doctor diagnosed it, reached her heart, and she died. Eleanor's arms were around her as she left her life behind. Her ears closed upon the sound of Eleanor's voice assuring her that once again they would manage their escape together, somehow: nothing, no one, would prevent them.

The Ladies left Plas Newydd together. Sarah was beside Eleanor as they walked arm in arm along the gravelled path and straight down the aisle of cedar trees. They wore their newly made habits of fine white cloth. Their faces were set towards a New country.

EPILOGUE

After Sarah's death, Robert Tighe came to settle her es-
tate. The house and the beautiful grounds did not in the
least interest him or stir his imagination. Furthermore, he
regarded Wales as an outpost on the edge of civilisation.
Nothing would persuade him to live and raise his sons in
such a barbaric place, not even for part of the year. So he
arranged with a land agent to sell the house for him.

In six months it was bought by two New recluses (as the
Ladies might have called them), Miss Amelia Lawley and
Miss Charlotte Andrewes, who had lived in the village for
some time. They made only one addition to the decor: a
large stuffed bear (of which Sarah would surely have
approved), which stood in the corner of the library until
they died. The Place was bought by General Isaiah Yorke
for the purpose of 'restoring' it. The entire front was
redone in Elizabethan style, with oak strips covering the
stone, thus burying the old beloved face of the house in
dark gloom. General Yorke built a new wing at the back,

changing the original form of the house. He constructed a New building, which he called the Hermitage, at the north-west end of the property.

There he lived, turning the house itself into a museum of relics of the Ladies: Eleanor's decorations, Chance's collar, the lovespoons, two beaver hats, Eleanor's tele-scope and Sarah's kaleidoscope, the vast collection of labelled gifts, and furniture, including the New bed.

Upon his death, a Liverpool cotton merchant, Mr G. H. Robertson, bought Plas Newydd and increased its gran-deur. He built two reception rooms, halls, bedrooms, and four bathrooms. Now it had become the mansion Eleanor had always thought it to be. In 1910 Robertson retired and sold the place to a man from Lincolnshire, who lived there until after the First World War. He found it hard to maintain the gardens. When the 'New' gazebo overlooking Hill Road fell into disrepair he had it taken down. Other buildings, the dairy, the bird cote, became rotten and were removed.

Then, for twelve years, Plas Newydd had what the Ladies would have considered fitting tenants. The Seventh Earl of Tamberville and his wife purchased it for use as a summer home. They made very few adjustments and occu-pied it only occasionally. When the Earl died, Llangollen's town council, upon the advice of the Bureau of Tourists, acquired the Place. Advertised in brochures and fully de-scribed in travel magazines and newspapers, Plas Newydd joined Dinas Bras, Valle Crucis, St. Collen's, and the Dee Bridge as a tourist attraction.

In the 1930s a stocky woman in her early seventies with grey close-cropped hair, Dr Mary Gordon, visited Dr Carl

Jung in Bollingen, Switzerland. During the unburdening of her troubled spirit to the eminent psychoanalyst, Dr Gordon described a place in her girlhood she was dreaming about, almost to obsession: the ruins of the Valle Crucis Abbey. Dr Jung decided she should return to Llangollen as part of her treatment.

She followed his advice. Though she had not been to her home village in fifty-six years she found her way easily through its 'sights' and streets. One early evening she walked to Plas Newydd, which she did not remember having visited before. In the dusk she wandered through the gardens, searching for the custodian to admit her to the mansion.

When she found him, an old man in a worsted suit and cap, he stared at her in amazement. To set his mind at rest she thrust out her hand to him.

'I am Doctor Gordon,' she said. 'I am hoping to be able to see the inside of the house.'

The custodian did not reply.

'I *am* sorry. I must have startled you.'

Still he said nothing.

'What's the matter?'

'For a moment there, ma'am, just for a moment, mind you, in the darkness and all, I took you for Lady Eleanor Butler.'

In 1936 Doctor Mary Gordon wrote a book about the Ladies. She said she had caught sight of them in their garden and had felt their presence in the State Bedroom. They were dressed in light-blue linen habits and fine muslin shirts. The three women, she reported, talked together until cockcrow. She saw that the Ladies' spirits were still in residence, and she believed they intended to remain as long as a shell of their New Place stood, a tree to which they had nailed a motto remained, a single shapely shrub survived.

Dr Gordon's book was published by Leonard and Virginia Woolf at their Hogarth Press in London.

The Ladies share a headstone, a four-sided, carved stone that rises above most of the other grave markers in St. Collen's graveyard. On the stone, contrary to Dr Gordon's prediction, these words are carved:

> JOB: BUT THEY STILL SHALL NO MORE
> RETURN TO THEIR HOUSE, NEITHER SHALL
> THEIR PLACE KNOW THEM NO MORE.

Yaddo Saratoga Springs.
Moody Beach, Maine.
Writers Workshop, Iowa City:
1981—1983.

ACKNOWLEDGEMENTS

For some facts and stories, which I have everywhere garbled, changed, or rearranged, I looked into the following books: *The Hamwood Papers*, edited by Mrs. G. H. Bell, and *Cross Roads in Ireland* by Padraic Colum, both volumes published in London by Macmillan in 1930. *Chase of the Wild Goose* by Mary Gordon, published by the Hogarth Press in 1936. *The Land of Wales* by Eilund and Peter Lewis, published in London in 1937 by B. T. Batsford. Mary Alden Hopkins's *Dr. Johnson's Lichfield* appeared in New York in 1952, published by Hastings House. *The Ladies of Llangollen* by Elizabeth Mavor, a most useful book, was published in London by Michael Joseph in 1971, and *Wales*, compiled by Jan Morris, a lovely small book by a veteran travel writer

211

and resident of Wales, was published in 1982 by Oxford University Press.

The story of Mrs French and the farmer's clipped ears is told in "The Tower" by William Butler Yeats.

ABOUT THE AUTHOR

Prominent critic and writer Doris Grumbach is a regular reviewer on National Public Radio and a member of the New York Book Critics Circle. She lives in Washington, D.C.